DIFFERENT DIRECTIONS

by

Sonny Collins

ISBN: 978-0-578-02087-7

Prairie Moon Publications
P. O. Box 236
Hillsboro, KS 67063

Printed in the USA

for

Trace & Fran

Also by SONNY COLLINS

Summer of the Stranger
Mouse Tails
Distant Dreams
Beneath a Western Sky
Please Take a Seat

Some writers take a single path

But I prefer different directions.

COMANCHE GARDEN

The two hikers never knew what hit them. Both men were climbing up through the granite boulders on the north side of Mount Pinchot when death came calling. The arrow whizzed silently through the air until it met its target. The man felt a sharp pain in his back seconds before he saw the protruding piece of wood, covered in blood, sticking out of his chest. No sound escaped his lips as he collapsed onto the rocks. The other man was higher up and did not see what had befallen his comrade. When he heard the sound of a body hitting the rocks, instinctively, he knew his friend had stumbled on the boulders. With just the slightest of smirks across his face he started to turn. The arrow caught him through the side of his neck, spinning him around. A second arrow tore through his Adams apple, choking all the breath out of his throat. The man was dead before he hit the ground. So began another beautiful day in the Wichita Mountains Wildlife Refuge of southwest Oklahoma.

****

Travis Penwadee was starting to feel old. At fifty, he was noticing that his body was slowing down and aching all over. He turned the truck onto the dirt road and then stopped in front of the locked gate. Travis hated the fences that crossed the landscape of the refuge, but he knew why they were needed, not just to help protect the animals, but also to keep people out of the restricted area of the park. He slowly got out of the truck, sorted through his keys until he found the one he needed and unlocked the gate. Swinging it open wide, he headed back to the truck and drove forward. There was no need to close the gate because he knew the rest of his crew would be close behind. It was their responsibility to make sure it was locked. Travis drove down the rutted, dirt road toward the granite mountains in front of him.

The day was going to be a scorcher. It was only ten in the morning and already hitting up into the high 90's. Travis was standing next to his truck when the others arrived. A big grin crossed his dark, round face. Travis waved as the two jeeps swung in beside him. Two passengers jumped out of each of the vehicles. They were all in their early twenties. It was obvious that all of the men were Native Americans, to be more precise, Comanche.

"When are you going to join the 21st Century and get one of these?" Billy Reedwood asked, patting the hood of his new red jeep.

"My old '72 Dodge gets me to wherever I want to go, and I don't have no big car payments like you boys," Travis grinned. "New cars are for the young, us older folks know how to waste our money in other ways."

"Yeah, old man, like hitting the bars every Friday and Saturday night," Billy laughed as the others did the same.

"I gave up the bottle for a better vice," Travis snickered. "Now I throw my money away on the slot machines over at the Casino in Lawton."

"Well, if you ever win big, I bet you'll buy a new truck," Billy added.

"Maybe."

The days work for the five men was hard and long. Not much talk was made between them as they each went about their task. Travis had been the foreman of this crew for more than two years. He liked the four young men, but had never grown really close to any of them. He knew they drank a lot and smoked a little pot whenever they had the chance. They did other things he didn't approve of as well. It wasn't his place to tell them what to do once they were away from the work site, besides; he had done some of the same when he was their age. As long as they put in a full days work, that was all he cared about. They were earning their money on this job. The five men were moving rocks to make a new trail. Travis had originally thought it was a waste of time and taxpayer dollars considering it was in a part of the refuge that wasn't open to the public, but the Park Superintendent had explained how it was for the rangers to take special guests on private excursions into the protected area and show how the wilderness was exactly as it had been hundreds of years before. That is, if one can overlook the boulder-lined path that was being made around the mountain.

"Hey, Old Man! I think I've found something." Billy was standing near a small ditch, covered with weeds and brush.

"It sure ain't you're brains," Travis called out. "The trail is not supposed to be that close to a drop off. What are you doing over there?"

"Had to take a leak. Come look at this!"

Travis cautiously walked over to where the young man was stooping low to the ground. As he approached Billy, he noticed the backpack tossed into the bushes below. "What's the big deal? Someone dumped their pack?"

"Look closer. I think it's covered in blood," Billy

whispered softly.

"Damn. I think you are right," Travis agreed. He glanced around to see where the others were. There was no sign of them.

"We better get back and report this to the police," Billy stated as he started to reach for the pack.

"Not a good idea to move stuff at a crime scene," Travis warned, "don't you ever watch television?"

Billy pulled his hand back and was starting to get up when he felt a strong arm wrap around his neck. Before he had time to struggle, a knife slit across his throat from ear to ear. Blood gurgled up inside of his mouth as he was released from the powerful grip. Billy fell into the dirt, grasping with both hands at his throat, trying to stop the flow of warm liquid. In terror, he tried to scream, but only bubbles of crimson came forth from his mouth. With pleading eyes, he looked up at Travis for help. The older man just smiled down at him, wiping his knife clean. As the realization of who had killed him set in, Billy's lungs burst, having filled with blood.

"Sorry, Boy." Travis pushed the lifeless body over into the same ditch with the backpack. Billy had been hinting at things lately and it wasn't worth the risk as far as Travis was concerned. He then realized his work wasn't done just yet. The other guys wouldn't leave the area without first searching for their missing friend. Travis knew it was time for a new crew. Darkness fell across the land as stars filled a glorious night sky. Another day done.

****

"Are you sure this is the right way to go?" Lisa asked again. David looked at his sister with disdain. "We aren't even supposed to be here."

"Calm down, Sis, this will be a lot more fun than camping

10

out in the Charon Gardens Wilderness area. Don't you want to see some stuff no one ever gets to see?"

"Not if it means getting caught, or even worse, lost."

"I promise you. We aren't lost. The old rock quarry should be just over this next hill." David Pomaroy was always sure of himself. The well muscled, blond teen prided himself on the fact that he could instinctively tell what direction he was facing at all times. He and his sister had been on camping trips to the park ever since they were young kids. This was their first trip without the folks. They had convinced their parents to let them go on their own. What their parents didn't know was the fact that they had plans to meet up with some friends and party all weekend.

"Are you sure that Chris and Nick know how to find this place?" Lisa inquired, tired of her older brother's air of superiority. He was only a senior to her junior in school.

"I told you. They have been here before. This is going to be the greatest place to camp. No one will bother us because this entire side of the park is off limits. That's why we left the car over at Sunset picnic area and hiked here."

"I still don't like the fact that we climbed under the fence. The sign very clearly said to keep out!"

"If you were one of the guys, I'd be calling you a wimp about now."

Lisa shot him the finger. "I won't even say what I'd like to call you."

"Like I care," David mocked. He then climbed up a small rock wall and turned back toward his sister. "Get up here. This is it."

Lisa was impressed as she walked around the pool of water that was surrounded by granite cliffs. Chris and Nick had already put up a tent at the far end of the quarry and were waiting for them. Even though the two boys were her brother's friends, Lisa had a crush on Nick. Unfortunately, so did Chris. Lisa had tried to tell her brother, but he always brushed off the subject, saying they were just close buddies. He simply didn't know how close.

"We got beer and hotdogs, what could be better?" Nick yelled out.

"Some hot chicks," David retorted as he and his sister walked into the camp. "I suppose I'll have to settle for a beer."

"Unless incest counts," Chris laughed, pointing at Lisa.

"You disgust me."

"Come on, let's not fight. Let's have some fun," Nick said, pulling Lisa away from the others. "Just ignore Chris. He's more bark than bite."

"You should know." Sarcasm was in her voice.

"Don't believe all the rumors. I'm not even going to try to speak for Chris, but I like girls as much as your brother does."

"That's good to hear. There might be hope for us yet." The words were no sooner out of her mouth than she regretted saying them.

"You like me?" Nick smiled.

"Shut up! Let's join the others and see how the night goes."

The beer flowed freely. Lisa realized it must have been quite a feat for the two guys to drag the three beer filled ice-chests up to the quarry. They had to have made several trips. It was a wonder they had not gotten caught. Her brother would have no doubt been a big help to them had he not brought her along. At least David didn't mind including her on his outings. Despite a few stupid arguments, they had always been very close. Lisa drank another beer and enjoyed the sounds of crickets and frogs chirping near the water. The day had been hot, but evening shadows were starting to fall, bringing a cool breeze.

"Let's go swimming," David said, pointing to the pond in front of them. "It has to be deep. It was a rock quarry back in the old days. I'll bet we can dive off the rocks by the cliff."

"I don't know, David. You can see the tops of boulders sticking out of the water. And look at all that seaweed," Lisa noted. She always had to be the practical one.

"Good point," Nick smiled, joining David near the water. "But it looks clear enough at this end to swim in. A nice dip in the water would feel good."

"We didn't bring suits," Lisa asserted.

"Who needs suits? We're all friends. Let's go skinny-dipping," Chris laughed as he sat on a rock and started taking off his hiking boots.

"You don't care, do you?" David asked his sister for approval.

Lisa shook her head in resignation and grinned at the three guys in front of her. "It doesn't bother me any, but don't expect me to join you. I'm just going to sit here and watch."

"Ewww, she likes to watch," Chris cracked wisely as he stood up and pulled his shirt off. He then faced directly toward Lisa and dropped his shorts, boxers and all. "Now you can say you've seen a real man."

"And after you get in the water she'll see how a man shrinks back to a boy," David laughed, giving Nick a high-five.

"You guys are only jealous," Chris replied, stepping out onto one of the rocks at the waters edge. "You chickens coming?"

David and Nick both stripped down to bare skin and

joined their friend. Lisa hated to admit it, but they all looked rather good to her. Tight butts, six-pack abs and nice looking torsos. Even her brother was not exactly repulsive. She watched as the three guys slowly slipped into the dark waters and swam around. They looked like they were having fun as they splashed one another, and for the briefest of moments, Lisa thought about joining them, but decided she wasn't quite as brave as the guys were. She drank another beer and watched as Nick and Chris climbed out of the water on the opposite side. Her eyes were drawn to Nick's mid-section, but not for the reason one would have thought.

"Get out of the water, David!" Lisa yelled at her brother as she stood up and pointed at Nick. "You have leaches on you!"

Nick looked down and started slapping at the little bloodsuckers that were attached to his inner thigh. Panic spread quickly as Chris realized there were some on his left buttocks. Both boys were jumping up and down, screaming in terror. Lisa rushed over to where David was coming out of the water. He was laughing as he quickly checked himself over and found nothing.

"How's my back, Sis?"

Lisa gave him a fast once over. "You don't have any that I can see. Are you going to help them? They are freaking out."

"Calm down, guys," David hollered. "What a bunch of wimps. Get over here and I'll show you how to get them off. They are like big ticks."

Nick and Chris came running over the rocks and brush, avoiding the water at all cost. Lisa grimaced as they joined her and David. She could see blood coming from one of the wounds where Chris had pulled a leach off. Both guys stood in front of David, afraid to touch the slimy invaders.

"What do we do?" Nick asked through gritted teeth.

David kept smiling before motioning for Lisa. "Let me have your lighter." Lisa didn't think David knew she smoked, but rather than argue with him about the point, she pulled the lighter from her pocket and handed it to him.

"What are you doing?" Chris whined as David pushed the flame toward his friend's butt.

"Fire makes them let go and they fall off," David pointed out, holding the lighter against one of the leaches. Just as he said, the creature dropped to the ground.

"What about the one on my privates?" Nick asked hesitantly.

"I guess you better be extra careful," David grinned, handing him the lighter. Nick was shaking uncontrollably as he burned away the rest of the fiends from his body.

"How was that for some excitement?" David laughed after they had all made sure they were free of the leaches.

"That was the grossest thing I've ever had happen to me," Chris shuddered, rubbing at the bites on his backside. David turned to Lisa and pointed back at Chris. "I told you he would shrink up to nothing."

"That's not even funny!" Chris sneered. Lisa had to laugh.

"Come on, guys! This is supposed to be a party. Grab some beers and let's pull out the cards. I'm ready for some Texas hold'em." David never seemed to let anything faze him.

"Yeah, Chris. This whole trip was your idea anyway. Let's have some fun," Nick tried to appease his buddy.

The standard smart aleck grin came back as Chris turned to the only female among them. "So Lisa. How well do I stack up against these two in the male anatomy department?"

"Oh, shut up! I can't believe you have such a one track

mind. Get over yourself," Lisa acted out mock indignation. "Besides, from what I hear, you are the one who is probably memorizing the two of them."

"Touché," Nick laughed.

"Ha! Ha! Real funny," Chris smirked, but not before taking a good look at David and Nick.

The guys swiftly got back into their clothes and returned to drinking, playing cards and making jokes. Lisa knew better than to stay out of this game, she joined in and gave them a run for their money. By the time they decided to start a fire and cook the hotdogs, all four of them were decently drunk. Darkness meant nothing to them as they stumbled around and kept right on drinking. Chris was the first to pass out, but not before making a meager pass at David, who just ignored him. They had all grown up together and accepted each others faults.

"I'm turning in," David finally stated, crawling into the tent.

"I'm staying out here a little longer," Lisa informed him, turning to Nick. She knew from the way he was looking at her what was going to happen.

"Let's go for a walk," Nick whispered, helping Lisa to her feet. The ground seemed wobbly, or it could have been the effects of the liquor. She didn't care.

"You looked good earlier," Lisa giggled as they made their way to some huge boulders. "Even if you did scream like a girl when those leaches got on you."

"Now, in my own defense, that was not what I wanted sucking on me," Nick grinned, pulling Lisa close to his side.

"How about me sucking your lips right off your face?" Lisa laughed, not even realizing how ridiculous she sounded.

Nick didn't care either as he pulled her close to him and kissed her hard on the lips. They both almost lost their balance, but neither one stopped kissing the other. Lisa felt his hand wrap around her waist as she held to him tightly. They slid down to the ground in a warm embrace as their kiss grew more passionate. This was a night they would never forget.

Travis Penwadee watched the two teens from the shadows.

****

Carla Reedwood was not happy. Her son, Billy, along with the three other men he worked with, had been gone for over a week. She didn't care that their boss said he overheard them planning to go down to Mexico. It wasn't like her son to not contact her. Billy may have been a little wild at times, but he had never vanished before without a word to anyone. Carla was tired of waiting for a call. She needed to find out for herself exactly what had been said. She felt no apprehension as she pulled her truck up in front of the trailer of Travis Penwadee. They had both been in the same class together at the Indian school in Lawton. It was Travis who had given her son a job when no one else would. Even though they had not socialized much through the years, she still considered Travis a friend. She was a little surprised to see that he was awake so early on a Saturday morning.

"What brings you way out here in the boondocks?" A jovial Travis asked from his seat on the front porch of the trailer.

Carla got out of the vehicle and stepped up next to where the stocky man sat. "This thing with Billy is driving me nuts. If he had gone to Mexico with those other guys, he'd have called me by now. Are you sure it was all four of them talking about going? Billy always was leery of Mexico because he was afraid that with his being an Indian, they might think he was Mexican and not let him back across the

17

border."

Travis offered Carla a chair. She sat down awaiting his reply. "It's like I told our boss, I don't really know where they went. I just heard them talking about driving down there and getting some women. You know how young men will talk. When they didn't show up for work the next morning, I simply chalked it up to hormones and that they had decided to go. I'm sure you don't have anything to worry about. They are probably having a blast on some beach right now."

"I just can't believe Billy wouldn't call and let me know he was alright. He knows I don't care about any of that other stuff."

Travis took Carla by the hand. "I wouldn't worry your pretty little head about it. Billy is bound to show up sooner or later."

Carla shook her head in disagreement. She knew something wasn't right, but it was obvious Travis had no idea where the guys were. She looked at the mountain that was south of the trailer. "Isn't that Bakers Peak?"

Travis nodded in agreement. "My property line backs up to the park. Makes it kind of nice to have all this peace and quiet out here."

"Do you get many hikers crossing onto your property?" Carla asked.

Travis chuckled. "I hope not. This side of the park is closed off to the public, although there are always a few adventuresome souls who feel they have to climb Bakers Peak or Mount Pinchot. I chased off some guys on mountain bikes a few weeks ago."

"I never understood why anyone would want to climb any of these God forsaken mountains. Between the heat, rattlesnakes and the cactus, I never saw the appeal."

"That's because you grew up here," Travis pointed out. "But people come from all over the world to see our big granite boulders and wild buffalo herd."

"One thing is for certain, you must like it. How can you stand living so far off the main road? You are literally out in the middle of nowhere." Carla tried to muster a smile, looking around at the dense post oak forest east of the trailer.

"It suits me," Travis grinned. "Back in one of the canyons that cross from the park to my property is the most beautiful spring and a natural garden, full of wild flowers and ferns. I go there often when I want to get close to nature. It is my own private retreat. I keep all my hunting trophies there."

"Sounds like a nice place, you'll have to take me there sometime," Carla stated.

"Who knows, it might calm your nerves a bit," Travis remarked with a sly wink. "Would you like to see it right now?"

Carla stood up. "It sounds lovely, but I really have to be going. I've got an appointment with the Sheriff in an hour. I was hoping you would be able to give me some new leads, but you can't give me what you don't have. You can't blame me for trying. Thanks so much, Travis."

"I hope you find your boy." The man didn't even stand up as Carla went back to her truck and drove away.

Carla had barely driven around a rugged mass of rocks and out of sight of the trailer when something caught her eye in the narrow canyon below the dirt road. Something was shining brightly in the reflection of the sun. Carla slowed down and covered her eyes to get a better look. What she saw gave her a chill. It looked like the remains of a wrecked jeep. And it was red.

****

Lisa had a slight headache as she crawled out of the tent.

19

David and Nick were directly behind her. Nick went over to where Chris had passed out and gave him a swift kick in the butt. That woke him up.

"Did I sleep outside all night?" Chris suddenly realized.

"Duh. You passed out and were dead to the world. We couldn't have woke you up if we had wanted to," David stated.

"You guys probably took advantage of me," Chris whined.

"You wish," David laughed as he went over to the pool of water. "Anyone for a morning swim?"

Nick and Chris both shuddered at the thought.

"I say we do some hiking. Are we leaving the tent here or camping somewhere else tonight?" Lisa asked.

"I know this really great canyon on the north end of the park. It has a spring and everything. I figured we'd hike to it and spend the night there." Nick had apparently broken the rules before.

Chris finally smiled. "We found the place the last time we were here. There aren't any leaches where we swam. There are all these bones and animal skulls hanging in the trees. I think it's some kind of Indian thing. The canyon is awesome."

The four teens went about the job of breaking camp. The boys carried backpacks filled with the tent, sleeping gear and the rest of their supplies. Lisa was given the pack filled with the food. Since they had drank all the beer, it was decided to leave the ice-chests and retrieve them on the way back. There was not a cloud in the sky as the four friends started their journey. The yellow and white granite boulders looked almost golden in the morning sunlight. The path that Nick took was rough, but considering there was no actual trail, it could have been worse. They headed north toward Bakers

Peak.

****

Travis had a strange feeling in the pit of his stomach. After Carla Reedwood had left, he found himself thinking about those kids up at the old rock quarry. If they had broken camp and gone back to their car they would be safe. But if they had continued on into the protected area, all bets were off. He decided he had better go up there and find out which choice they had made. His knee popped as he climbed into the beat up truck. He knew he was getting too old for this kind of stuff. Starting the truck, he wondered what the day was going to bring.

****

The three women rode their bikes single file along the dirt road. They were all in their early thirties, still fit and trim from daily workouts and weekend bike rides together. Their husbands had decided to race and had taken another route on one of the paved roads through the park. The women had decided to follow the dirt road that skirted the north boundary. They were coming around a narrow curve when they saw the truck barreling down on them. One of the women was able to throw herself into the rocks as the truck slammed into her two friends. Bikes and bodies crumpled seconds before being ejected over the side of the deep ravine. The truck made a screeching stop. The woman realized that she had injured her leg when she slammed into the boulders. She slowly pulled herself up and started walking to the other side of the road to check on the condition of her friends. The broken bodies in the ravine made the woman gasp. She turned back to the truck, waiting for the driver to get out and help after such a senseless accident. A thought suddenly hit the woman. Had it been an accident? The truck went into reverse and before the woman could move, slammed into her.

21

She was knocked down onto the rocky road. She could feel the cuts in her hands as she tried to get up. The truck hit her again. The woman lay there in a daze. Once again the truck pummeled the woman, this time driving right over her broken body. There was no movement from the woman because there was no longer any life left in her.

****

"Dammit! I can't find my car keys," Nick groaned, searching through his pack. The others were sitting around on boulders, eating granola bars.

"Where did you have them last?" Chris asked.

Nick put his hand to his head when he remembered where he'd left them. "I put them on one of the ice-chests this morning so that I wouldn't forget them."

"Nice going, dude," David laughed. "We'll get them on the way back."

Nick didn't care for that idea. "I'm not leaving my keys there until tomorrow. I'll go back and get them. Chris knows how to get to the canyon we are going to. I can catch up with you guys later."

"Are you sure you don't want us to wait here for you?" Lisa asked.

"That would just be wasting your time. You guys can go on and get the camp set up." Nick looked up at the hot noon sun. "I should only be two or three hours behind. We can all go swimming at the spring when I rejoin you."

"Sounds like a plan," David agreed.

"Are you sure you'll be able to find us?" Lisa wanted to know.

Nick grinned. "I'll probably get to the canyon before you do, especially with Chris leading you. Just remember, it's to the east of Bakers Peak."

"I know how to find it," Chris smirked.

"Then I'll meet you there." Nick grabbed his pack and started back in the direction from which they had come.

****

Carla Reedwood was having trouble catching her breath. She parked her truck in the shade of some trees and waited. The heat was stifling. When Travis Penwadee appeared in his pick-up, she ducked down in the seat. After he passed, Carla sat up and started her own vehicle. She hoped he hadn't noticed her truck in its hiding place off the road. Carla had been waiting for hours. She slowly followed behind Travis at a safe distance. He was obviously heading for the park. When she saw him pull off the road at the west entrance, she stopped her truck and waited. Travis didn't even glance in her direction as he got out and vanished into the brush. Carla parked her vehicle behind some bushes and then waited about ten minutes before getting out and walking down the side of the road to the other truck. It didn't go without her noticing that there were three mangled bikes in the back of the vehicle. She slowly made her way up the steep incline. A Department of Wildlife fence blocked her way. Carla wasn't going to let that stop her. She carefully crawled through the barbed wire. A cactus pricked her leg. Carla ignored the pain and made her way across an outcropping of rocks. Climbing to the top of the hill, she realized that this was the way to the old rock quarry. She wondered what Travis was up to. Could Billy and the other boys be there? She had to know what had happened to her son and it now seemed that Travis Penwadee knew more than he had let on. Carla made her way through the brush.

****

Travis noticed the three ice-chests right away. The fact that there was a set of keys left behind told him that the owners would be back. It also meant they had gone into the restricted zone. There was no telling in what direction they went or where they were heading, Travis realized. He might have been an Indian, but at his age, he knew he was in no condition to track a bunch of white kids into the wilderness. He thought about taking the keys to teach them a lesson, but then decided against it.

****

Nick was so glad to finally see the rock quarry ahead. It had taken him longer than he had thought to get back. The heat of the day was a real killer, radiating off the granite boulders that lay everywhere in the park. As Nick hiked around some piles of slate and found himself in front of the pool of water he couldn't help but grimace.

"You damn leach pond! Just wait until tonight when I'm swimming around in a nice clear spring and looking up at Bakers Peak." He yelled at the top of his lungs to nobody in particular. Nick just wanted the leaches to know how he felt.

Walking over to where they had left the ice-chests, Nick realized that his keys weren't there. Now he was really pissed. He glanced around in the dirt, hoping that someone may have knocked them off in all the bustle of packing up camp that morning. There was no sign of them. What was he going to do now? Nick debated about heading to his car and grabbing his cell phone so that he could call his parents and have them bring the extra set. That would only tick them off. Nick decided it would be better to simply return to the others. David and Lisa could take him and Chris back with them and then he could get the extra keys and have Chris drive him back to get his car tomorrow night.

Nick turned around to start back when he noticed something shiny hanging from a nearby tree branch. It looked like his keys. He grinned as he walked over and reached for them. It never occurred to him how they had gotten there. Nick grasped the keys as a shadow passed from behind him. Turning to see what had caused it, a rock smashed into his head, throwing him to the ground. Blood mingled in the dirt as Nick lost consciousness.

****

"Are you sure you can find this place?" David asked.

Chris shot him an icy glare. "I know where I'm going. There should be an old mine in this next canyon. We go north from there and cross the boundary fence and find the spring."

"I hope you are right. This heat is killing me," Lisa said, wiping the sweat from her brow. She looked around at the rugged expanse of hidden canyons behind them. The Wichita Mountains might not have been very tall, but no one could argue the fact that they were very misleading. What looked like an easy stroll often turned into a very strenuous hike. Lisa knew a lot of people had been hurt or lost in these mountains. After a while, each canyon looked the same. And that was on the side that all the tourists hiked. Lisa was having misgivings about this trip. She could still remember the time her family had hiked through the Narrows and saw a young climber fall to his death from one of the sheer rock walls. This place was not for the squeamish. There were a lot of places one could get hurt while climbing the granite boulders.

"I think I see the mine," Chris excitedly pointed down into the nearby canyon. "It's that dark hole over near those bushes."

David squinted his eyes for a better view. "You might be right. Let's go check it out." He turned to his sister. "Do you want to stay up here until we are sure?"

"I'm sticking with you guys. Just because I'm the girl, doesn't mean I don't want to check things out too."

David grinned at his sister. "Well then, come on." He started down the steep canyon, climbing over sharp, jumbled rocks and thick underbrush. Chris was right behind him.

Lisa didn't like the route they were taking and looked around for an alternative. As she suspected, there was a gentle, sloping path down into the canyon. She hiked along the rim until she came to a spot where she could hike down with ease. The guys laughed at her as she joined them at the bottom.

"Our way was more fun," David asserted.

"Judging by the scratches on both your legs, it felt better too," Lisa smiled.

"At least we beat you down," David declared.

"I didn't know it was a race."

Before David had a chance to exchange more zingers with his sister, Chris cut in, "Does anyone want to go exploring? Grab the flashlights."

"Isn't it closed up?" David asked, walking over to the dark hole in the side of the granite wall. "We used to go in the Pennington Mine when we were kids, but they blocked it off with iron bars years ago. Is this one still open?"

Chris shook his head up and down. "What is the point of closing off a mine tunnel in the part of the park that is closed to the public?"

"Are you sure we are still in the park?" Lisa asked. "I saw some metal stakes up on the rim and thought they might be boundary markers."

"What does it matter? Do you want to go in the mine or not?" Chris inquired.

Lisa headed for the entrance. "I'm not passing up a chance to go in a mine or a cave, ever."

David knew his little sis wasn't kidding. "She loves to go spelunking. Most girls are scared of the dark and hate getting dirty, not my sister."

The three explorers took off their packs and dug around until they had found their flashlights. David took the lead, followed by Lisa and Chris. The tunnel was barely tall enough for them to stand straight. The walls were solid granite. The floor was dry, but showed signs of once having been wet and muddy, probably during the spring rains. The tunnel was cut at a downward angle and curved, drawing them out of sight of the entrance. The flashlights put out plenty of light as the three continued down the narrow corridor. They finally came to a large room at the end.

"This is awesome. Why haven't you brought us here before now?" David asked Chris. "I'll bet this tunnel is three times longer than the Pennington Mine. We must have come at least three to four hundred feet into the side of this canyon."

"Nick and I found it on our last trip. We knew you and Lisa thought you had seen everything in the park and that is why we saved this for a surprise. Do you like?"

"Totally." David kept looking around, knowing there was no gold or silver, but still impressed with the work that had been done in the room.

"It's too bad Nick is missing this," Lisa noted, "but I have to admit, I'm glad we got to see it. Thanks for actually knowing how to get us here." She playfully jabbed Chris on the shoulder.

"At least you think I'm good for something," Chris chuckled. "Now are you guys ready to see the springs?"

"We're on it!" David exclaimed.

The three silently made their way back out of the mine. Upon reaching the entrance, the bright light almost blinded them. After letting their eyes adjust, they stepped back out into the Oklahoma heat. Putting their packs back on, they then marched down the canyon floor. The boundary fence was only a few hundred feet away from the mine. They climbed over it with ease. In what seemed like a matter of moments, the small canyon opened up into a much larger one. A towering grove of cottonwood trees looked over plush foliage of ferns. The water from the clear stream that meandered through the scene looked cool and refreshing.

"This is definitely the place," Lisa gasped with joy.

"You haven't seen nothing yet," Chris smiled. "Follow me."

Lisa and David went single-file as their friend led them around the bend. What they saw was much more than they ever expected. The spring apparently came out of the rocks at the end of the canyon. A small series of pools and waterfalls cascaded down through the boulders. It reminded Lisa of the double falls over by the Forty Foot Hole, but on a smaller scale. She was so mesmerized by the water that she didn't even notice the animal bones hanging from tree branches. Lisa threw off her backpack and started for the falls.

"Wait up, little Sis," David hollered. "Have you noticed anything out of the ordinary about this place?"

Lisa glanced around with a confused look on her face. "What are you talking about?" Before he could answer, she saw the bones. "How creepy."

Chris started laughing. "We told you there were weird animal skeletons scattered all over the place. I bet the Indians around here did this. Maybe we are on their Sacred Ground."

"Or maybe this is how they let everyone know this is the best swimming hole. I've read how the Indians mark a spot so that other Indians will know how to find it," David explained.

"Or maybe it's because the Comanche Indian who lives on this land likes to make wind-chimes out of bones." The three teens turned in shock to see a large Indian man behind them.

"We're so sorry, sir. We didn't mean to trespass," Lisa stammered.

"But you are. It would be best if you packed up your stuff and got out of here." The man told them.

"We don't want to sound disrespectful, but could we camp here for the night? Another member of our group is several hours behind us and is supposed to meet us here. He would not have a clue what do if he didn't find us at this spot," Lisa explained.

The man didn't seem to know how to answer. He finally spoke after a long moment of thought. "You can stay, but if your friend gets here before dark, I'd advise you to leave. Follow the creek a few miles and you will hit a road that will take you back around to the park."

"Thank you," Lisa offered. David and Chris nodded in agreement.

****

Carla watched from the rocks as Travis came out of the woods and went into his trailer. He was up to something. She had followed him most of the day. After he had come back from the rock quarry, he had returned to his place, but not before dumping the three bikes down into the same canyon where her son's jeep was. She wondered how many other bikes and vehicles were down there, hidden in the brush. It was the perfect dump site because no one ever used the drive to his place except for Travis. The realization that Billy and the others were probably not alive was finally starting to set in. Carla angered at the thought that Travis had killed them. Because she had to be certain, she could not leave her spot in the rocks above the trailer. She was going to watch and wait.

****

The evening sun was setting to the west as dark shadows fell through the canyons. Lisa sat in the waters of the clear pool. There were no leaches here. She enjoyed the cool water upon her skin. Since she was naked, she kept glancing around to make sure where the boys were. David and Chris were both climbing up one of the waterfalls and sliding down its smooth water-flume into the pool below. She couldn't get over how uninhibited boys were. The guys didn't even care that they were naked. Lisa had been a bit more bashful and had made them both turn their backs while she had undressed and slid into a pool. Then she had made them both keep at least fifty feet away from her private bath. Surprisingly, they had been good so far and not even glanced her way. They were having too much fun.

"Don't you think Nick should have gotten here by now?" Lisa yelled.

David turned toward her. "He knows these mountains. He'll be all right, even if he doesn't make it to us tonight. Don't worry so much."

"I wish we hadn't split up. It would be better if we were all together." Lisa also knew she was feeling this way because of the night before. Nick had seemed so into her. Now he'd been out of sight all day, maybe it was because he thought things had gotten a little out of hand and was embarrassed to be around her. She decided not to think about it as she swiftly climbed out of the water and wrapped her top around her. The guys never even noticed as she got dressed and then walked back to where they had put up the tent. A strange tinkling sound caused Lisa to shudder. The bones in the trees were hitting each other in the warm breeze.

30

Night was about to fall.

****

Travis Penwadee was troubled. He didn't like the fact that those kids were camping down at his favorite spot. A part of him wanted to go over and get rid of them, but there was something else bothering him. Carla Reedwood had been asking all the wrong questions. He suspected she was suspicious of him. She had seemed fine when she left, but he had begun to think differently as the day had progressed. Call it Indian intuition, or whatever you want to call it, but Travis had the feeling that he was being watched. More than once during the day he had thought he'd seen Carla's truck following him. Even now, he felt as though she was somewhere close by. It was very troubling. What if she had found out he had killed her Billy? Travis watched the sun go down from his trailer. Under the cloak of darkness he might be able to find out more.

****

David Pomaroy was on top of the world. He had climbed up the canyon wall and scaled one of the boulders. There was nothing but huge rocks below him on the other side. Chris sat at the waterfall, watching his friend. For years Chris had held a secret crush on David. Not even his closest friend, Nick, knew about it. Chris was aware it was hopeless. David was as straight as they came. It was enough to just be friends. Chris stood up to wave at David when the shot rang out.

"What the hell!" Chris hollered, turning in the direction from which the shot had echoed. He saw nothing. Turning back toward David, he was shocked to see his friend holding his side. Blood was pouring out from between his fingers. David looked down at him with bewilderment on his face.

Another shot rang out. The echo was deafening as Chris

31

watched in horror while his friend fell backwards off the boulder. David was gone. Chris did not have time to panic. He had to get to Lisa. Jumping down from the falls, Chris found himself stumbling on the rocks as he ran. Why had they let it get so dark? They should have already been back at the tent. Maybe then, they would have been safe. Once in the darkness of the big trees Chris felt a bit more hidden. Without a flashlight it would be hard for anyone to see him. He tripped over a fallen branch and fell to his knees. Chris knew he had to keep his wits about him if he was going to stay alive. Standing up slowly, he decided to pace himself. He calmly walked through the dark forest until he saw the light from the tent.

"Lisa! Turn off the light!" Chris yelled. Instead, she came out of the tent with the flashlight in her hand. "Turn it off!" Chris hollered again.

"What was that I heard? It sounded like a gunshot," Lisa stated.

Chris ran up to her, grabbing the light from her hand and switching it off. They both stood in darkness. "Someone just shot your brother."

"Oh my God!" Lisa screamed. Chris put his hand over her mouth.

"We've got to be quiet. Someone is out there with a gun and we aren't safe here."

"But what about David?" Lisa pleaded in a whisper.

"I'm so sorry, Lisa. He was up on a boulder and was shot twice. He fell off the mountain on the other side." Chris knew his words were hollow.

"I can't leave my brother. We have to see if he needs help," Lisa pleaded.

"Right now, we have to help ourselves. David would expect me to keep you alive. We have to leave camp, now!"

There was forcefulness in his voice that neither of them had ever heard before.

"What are we going to do?" Lisa asked calmly.

"I've got an idea. We'll try to sneak back to the mine and spend the night there. I noticed a bunch of bushes and tumbleweed around the entrance. I think I can camouflage it when we get there. In the morning we can try to figure out what to do. Are you with me?"

"Do I have a choice?" Lisa asked, regretting the fact that she sounded sarcastic when that was not what she meant.

Chris ignored her. "Stick close behind me."

****

Nick finally came to. He wished he hadn't. A scream could not escape his lips because of the gag around his mouth. If only whoever had done this could have covered his eyes as well. He was in water clear up to his neck. Even in the murky darkness he knew where he was. Somehow he had been immersed in the pool of the rock quarry. Quickly realizing that his hands were bound and tied behind his back as well as his feet and legs, Nick started to panic. There was no telling how long he had been like this. As his eyes adjusted to the darkness, he could make out how the rope around his neck was tied to a cable that was attached to the side of the cliff and went across the water over his head to a boulder on the opposite side. He realized it was at such an angle, that if he struggled too much, the rope holding him up out of the water would slide down, dragging him under. Tears filled his eyes. Then it hit him. Blood from the wound on the side of his head was dripping into the water. Nick wanted to cry out as he felt movement on his body. Leaches were all over him.

****

Lisa hated to admit it, but she was glad that Chris had

taken charge. This was a side of him she had never expected. Chris had always followed along with whatever Nick and David had done. She would have actually thought of him as a coward who would run at the first sight of trouble. It was such a shock to realize that he had rushed to her rescue instead of thinking about himself. Chris was more of a man than Lisa had ever given him credit for.

"I'm sorry I ever made fun of you," Lisa spoke softly. She was leaning up against his chest as they lay together on the dark floor of the mine.

"If we get out of this alive, you can make fun of me all you want," Chris tried to laugh. There was no fun in his voice like usual.

"Why would anyone be after us? Do you think it could have been a hunter that accidentally shot David?" Lisa asked.

"Maybe once, but they shot him twice. Whoever did it, knew what they were doing. I keep wondering about that Indian dude. With all those bones hanging in the trees on his place, maybe he's into some kind of weird Indian occult shit."

"When it gets light, I have to go back and make sure about my brother. I keep wondering if he could be hurt and injured out there. I can't leave until I find out, one way or the other."

"I figured as much. We'll climb along the fence line to avoid going back down in that canyon. I think we can sneak around to the other side of the boulder where David fell."

"Thanks for being such a good friend, Chris. I always took you for granted and I shouldn't have. I know how much you love David and Nick."

"Just go to sleep. We have a tough day ahead," Chris observed.

****

Sunlight slipped across the land as Nick shivered with fear. He couldn't understand why he had no feeling in his fingers. It was as if they weren't there. In the light of day he could better make out how the rope was tied around his neck and waist in such a way as to keep from choking him. Why would anyone want him to suffer this way? The leaches covered the lower half of his body and were working their way up. Nick grimaced as he felt something moving inside his ear. As a leach crawled up his face, Nick could take it no more. He started thrashing and moving about spastically. It turned out to be a fatal mistake. The rope slid along the cable wire. Nick sank beneath the surface of the water with no way of getting out. The more he struggled, the deeper he went. The last things he saw were the bodies of four Indian men anchored to the bottom of the quarry with chains and rocks as his lungs filled with water.

****

Travis Penwadee knew what had to be done. He grabbed his pistol from the night stand and went into the living-room. A quick glance at his possessions gave him an idea. He took down the spear hanging on the wall that his grandfather had made for him as a child. It was as sharp as a knife. Travis placed the gun in the side of his belt and made sure the knife he always carried was still strapped to the other side. When he had snuck out of the trailer the night before, he had seen Carla Reedwood. She had gone toward his canyon. He knew she was waiting in the woods for him. There was also the fact that those stupid kids were still out there somewhere. As he came out into the morning sun, Travis felt like a Comanche Warrior from the old days. He carried the spear at his side as he vanished into the forest.

****

"Are you certain this is the place, Chris?" Lisa asked, looking from her viewpoint on the boulder at the rocks below.

"He was standing right where you are when he was shot. He had to have fallen down there," Chris stated. He glanced around, not liking the fact that they were easy targets. "We need to get down off the rim."

Lisa grabbed his arm. "Oh my God. Look at that boulder down there. It's covered with blood."

Chris saw it. But the body was gone. He realized this was no ordinary killer. "Lisa, we have to get out of here. David is gone and there is no telling what has happened to Nick. You and I need to get to the police and let them figure this all out. This could be some kind of a deranged serial killer for all we know."

"You're right. We need to get away," Lisa agreed as she started back down off the boulder. Chris was directly behind her when a gunshot rang out. The bullet hit the rocks between them. Chris jumped, pushing Lisa down with him. The two rolled off the rocks and into a pile of brush and weeds.

"Are you all right?" Chris whispered, laying low on the ground beside her. Lisa only nodded her head as she looked at him. "We need to make a run for the trees. It will be harder for them to see us there. Whatever happens, don't look back, just keep running. I'll be right behind you. Run!"

The two stood up and darted over the boulders as though they had been born to the wilderness. With unexpected speed and agility, they maneuvered their way down into the canyon and to the cover of the cottonwoods. They didn't stop running until they reached their tent. Both of them stopped in their tracks at the scene before them. The tent had been torn to shreds and blood was everywhere.

****

Carla saw the boy and the girl at the campsite. She was between them and Travis Penwadee. He was coming through the woods, armed to the hilt. Carla eased herself behind a huge tree and waited. Even though she had been up all night, her mind was as clear as could be. If he was the one who had done it, Travis was going to have to answer for killing her son and his friends. She carefully pulled out the revolver that Billy had given her for protection. As Travis walked by, Carla swung herself out, pointing the gun at the man's back.

"Where is my Billy?" Carla yelled.

Travis stopped and slowly turned toward her. It was obvious he felt stupid for letting her sneak up on him so easily. "Calm down, Carla. You don't need that gun. Let's talk about this like reasonable people."

"Just tell me the truth," Carla ordered, moving in closer to the man. "Is Billy dead?"

"I had to kill him and the others," Travis admitted hesitantly. "But there was a good reason for me to do it. I did it..." Travis never finished his sentence because as he was saying it, he spun the spear around, knocking the gun from Carla's grip. In the next second, he jabbed at her, the spear slicing into her arm.

"Help me!" Carla screamed at the top of her lungs. She could see the two teens running in her direction.

"I have to end this, Carla," Travis stated calmly as he picked up her gun. He threw the bloody spear off to the side.

****

Lisa and Chris watched in horror as the big Indian knocked the gun from the woman's hand and then stabbed her in the arm. When she screamed for help, they knew she was in as much trouble as they were. Despite all their fears, a rush of adrenalin propelled them forward to help this endangered soul.

****

Travis Penwadee was really not that concerned about the two teens running in his direction. He had more important business to take care of. It was something he realized he should have done the moment the killings had started. He knew how bad it would have looked if they ever found out an Indian had been killing people in the park. He loved the Wichita Mountains too much to let that happen, so he had covered up most of the crime scenes and disposed of vehicles and such. A missing person never merited as much attention as a dead body. He realized his biggest flaw was the fact that he had let the killings go on longer than they should have. It was time for the killing to stop.

"It's over, Carla." He aimed the gun at the woman's head.

Travis never pulled the trigger. A pain like none he'd ever known shot through his body as the spear tore through his stomach. Travis went to his knees before falling onto his side. His own spear had done him in. By way of foggy eyes, he saw Carla standing over him, and then the two teens, then he saw the other one. He knew a blond boy, covered in bloody strips of cloth cut from the tent, had killed him. Apparently the injured boy had hid out all night under the boulders. When danger seemed imminent, the boy had reacted in the only way he knew how. Travis laughed to himself at his own folly. He would simply be another Indian killed by a white man. A boy at that.

"You gave me no choice!" The young man yelled down at him. "You were going to kill her." A change came over his angry face. The kid suddenly mellowed. "I'm so sorry. I didn't mean to hurt anyone. You made me do it."

With his last breath, Travis said, "I forgive you."

****

Carla Reedwood watched from the comfort of her porch swing as the sun went down. It had been over a month since the death of Travis Penwadee. Carla knew it had been a stroke of luck that the three surviving teens had confirmed her story that Travis had tried to kill them all and had confessed to killing his work crew. The only thing that bothered Carla was the fact that she would never know where Billy was buried. No one in the town of Cache understood how much she would miss her son and his buddies. Carla stood up and stepped down from the porch of her ranch house. She knew where she needed to go to meditate. A brisk fall breeze blew as Carla went around to the back of the house and stepped into her garden. Friends from town had often wondered how she was able to grow such exotic plants and roses in a desert land. Carla bent down at her newest flower bed. An old Comanche Shaman had told her the secret. The Shaman had told her she needed to grow things with a green thumb. She carefully pulled some items out of her pocket and dug a hole to bury them in. Billy and his friends would no longer be able to supply her with what she needed. Too bad Travis had finally figured everything out and ruined it all. Oh, well, she had done fine on her own, even though she still needed practice with her shooting. Her skills at running bikers down had no equal, she thought to herself as she covered the hole with dirt.

"Oops, this little fella' is still sticking up." Carla realized it was the last of her special items as she poked the human thumb back down into the fertile soil of her Comanche garden.

BROKEN DREAMS

The 'Thirsty Mule' was the only bar in town. Rhonda had worked there half her life. She was pushing forty, single and not happy about either. Sometimes she asked herself why she stayed at a dead-end job in a one horse town. That's when Cody walked in. That all too familiar swagger as he stepped up to the bar and gave a quick wave to the fella's over at the pool table. His eyes twinkled as he gave Rhonda a quick wink and ordered a beer. She shook her head and poured him a drink. The man had blown into town three years before as a guest singer at the bar and never left.

"When we gonna' hear you sing something again, Cody?" Rhonda couldn't help but ask, already knowing the answer would be the same as it had been every night for years.

"You know I don't like singing other folks songs. When I write something new I'll get back up on that stage and let you hear it first."

Rhonda had heard that too many times to believe it anymore. In the beginning she thought he was simply suffering a case of writers block, but after three years, she had come to realize it was much more than that. She knew after he had a couple rounds of beer he'd be reliving his glory days to anyone who would listen. Another story she knew by heart. Cody had been a much sought after songwriter in Nashville. A lot of old hits had his name attached. It was when he tried to make a career singing his own songs that he fell on hard times. Life on the road and too many small bars had taken their toll on his talent. His inspiration was gone. Rhonda had once hoped she'd be the one to bring it back, but that was another dream lost.

"What say we do a little two-step when you get a break?" Cody grinned, downing his beer, knowing it would be quickly filled up again.

"Have I ever turned you down?" Rhonda rolled her eyes.

"I still say I'm going to marry you someday and take you away from all of this." He flailed his arms wildly about, almost losing his balance.

"Easy does it, cowboy. You better grab a seat before the floor grabs you," Rhonda ordered.

Cody plopped himself in a chair at the bar and leaned over. "You are still going to marry me, aren't you?"

Rhonda was getting tired of always telling him yes, and having the end results being the fact that she never ended up with a ring. The game they played was beginning to get old. If she wasn't so dang in love with the bum she would have left a long time ago. But that was her fate. For good or bad, she loved the broken down troubadour with all her heart.

A couple of the guys asked Cody to play pool, which he was more than willing to oblige, knowing they'd be buying him the drinks. He waved to Rhonda as he headed over to the tables. She knew that would keep him occupied for a while. It would also give her time to think. Her escape had been planned for weeks now, but suddenly she wasn't so sure of herself. Could she actually get in her car and drive away from the town she had lived her entire life? Everything she owned was loaded in the little trailer she'd bought that morning. The bigger question was, would she be able to leave Cody behind? She would have asked him in a second if she actually thought he'd go with her, but she knew he'd make excuses about not being able to leave until he'd written a new song. A song she had realized was never going to come.

Cody raised a beer to Rhonda when he caught her glancing toward him. She smiled before turning away. The bar was going to be clean and tidy before she left. It was a decision made at the realization that she would never be coming back. Rhonda felt a tear trickling down her cheek. She wiped it away, hoping no one had noticed. That could be the reason bars are dark, so others can't see the pain or hurt in the lives of the patrons. It was a thought that had crossed her mind more than once. Rhonda busied herself with arranging bottles and getting everything in order. When the place was locked up at closing time, she was hitting the road. It didn't really matter where she ended up as long as it wasn't Texas.

"Penny for your thoughts," Cody grinned, strolling back to his seat at the bar.

"You drink too much."

"Why else would I be at a bar?"

"I'd like to think it was to see me."

"You're like the dessert. Worth waiting for in the end."

Rhonda laughed to herself. She knew they could banter like that all night long. If only she thought there was some truth to the sweet lies he told her. It gave her room to hesitate about her plans. She then noticed the guitar leaning against the wall. Maybe if she gave him one last chance.

"Why don't you play us a little something?"

Cody looked at the instrument and shook his head. "Got to have some words to go with the tune."

"So, does that mean you have a melody already?"

"Have a tune ready to go, just waiting for the words to follow."

"I think three years is a little long to wait." Rhonda had not meant to sound so sarcastic, but it didn't even faze Cody. He either ignored the double meaning or didn't catch it.

The opening of the entrance door drew their attention away from each other. A young man stepped into the bar, hesitant in his steps; as if he wasn't sure he wanted to be there. He slowly made his way to a booth in the corner and sat waiting.

"Obviously a city fella'," Rhonda smiled, "doesn't realize he's supposed to order drinks here at the bar. I'll go take his order."

"Don't flirt too much. I don't want anyone stealing my girl."

Rhonda went over to ask the young man what he wanted. It didn't surprise her that he ordered a pitcher of beer. She filled his order before returning back to her spot at the bar. Cody had waited patiently, apparently curious about their new guest. He sipped his beer before speaking.

"What do you think his story is?"

Rhonda figured it was the same as everybody else's. "He seems really down. There was sadness in his eyes. Doubt he wants to be bothered by anyone. He said when that pitcher is empty he wants another. I wish people would realize they can't drown their sorrows. Once you sober up, the problem is still the same until you solve it." She then turned directly to Cody. "Or in your case, ignore it."

Cody only grinned, taking another sip of his beer. He then turned his attention back to the young man in the corner. Rhonda went about her business of filling drinks, wondering why Cody seemed so interested in the new guy. Not that he wasn't one to talk with total strangers. There wasn't a person in the world that Cody didn't like. Especially when he was drinking. She wasn't at all surprised when he got up and strolled over to the booth. One would have thought she had been clear about the fact that the young man wanted to be left alone. Not that it mattered to Cody. She watched him plop down in the booth across from the other man. A deep conversation seemed to ensue. A part of her was glad Cody had found someone to pre-occupy himself with. It gave Rhonda time to address her own issues. Only a few more hours and the place would be closing up for the night.

Rhonda then noticed the young man getting up and leaving. He stepped out of the bar and was gone. She looked back over to see Cody sitting there, pouring beer from the pitcher into his glass. He was probably never going to change. All the more reason for her to leave. It wasn't the drinking she minded. Cody was a fun drunk. Not a mean bone in his body. It was the fact that he'd let his dreams die. She knew she could have put up with anything as long as there was a dream to follow.

The door opened again. The young man walked back over to Cody and spoke a few moments, never sitting down, and then quickly left. Rhonda had to wonder what that was all about. The guy was probably pissed because Cody was drinking his beer. She was about to go over and ask about it, when she noticed Cody pulling a pencil and some paper from his pocket. He was actually writing something down. There was no sense bothering him while he was busy with another distraction.

It was almost closing time before Cody finally returned to the bar. There was something different about the cocky grin that crossed his face. Rhonda wondered why? He didn't give her time to think about it as he grabbed her and planted a big kiss on her lips. She knew that was out of the ordinary.

"What's come over you?"

Cody wiggled his eyebrows playfully. "I'm not fooling this time. We're getting married." He then pulled a tiny box from his pocket, handing it to her.

Rhonda was almost afraid to open it, for fear it wouldn't be what she was hoping. But it was. A small diamond ring sparkled, even in the dim lights of the bar. She could hardly believe her own eyes as she put the ring on her finger. All her plans were dashed to pieces, but she no longer cared. Being stuck in Texas was a small price to pay for being with the man she loved.

Cody wasn't finished. "Will you move to Nashville with me? I'm ready to start writing again."

There was no containing the excitement in her voice. "I'm packed and ready to go. Can we leave tonight?"

A look of surprise crossed his face as Cody began to realize what he could have lost. Rhonda could see it in his expression as she covered him in kisses. She knew that his sudden decision was of his own making, and not because he'd found out she was leaving. It was all the sweeter with that knowledge.

"I always told you when I wrote a new song we'd leave this town in the dust. Do you want to hear what I wrote?"

"I've waited a long time for this."

"When I'm done, we're getting in your car and heading for a brand new adventure. Are you with me?"

"Always."

Cody then went over and grabbed the guitar. The room grew silent as he got up on the stage and started strumming a sweet ballad. His voice began in almost a whisper, but grew stronger as he hummed the tune. Then he began to sing and Rhonda knew all her wishes were about to come true. She listened proudly to her man's song.

BROKEN DREAMS

I could tell it was the first time
He'd ever been in a bar
The young man picked out a booth
The darkest one by far,

I ordered another beer
As I watched him from across the room
He ordered several drinks
And then downed them like a flume,

In his face there was such sorrow
He would never drown it in a drink
So I went over and sat across from him
And said this is what I think:

You're too young to be wasting time
Feeling sorry in your sorrows
Before you know it you've wasted years
And lost all of your tomorrows,
The only time you really have
Is the time you're wasting here
Life is out there for the living
Only broken dreams live in here.

His hands began to tremble
In his voice there was a shake
He said his life was already over
Everything he did was a mistake,

He said he wasn't good enough
To please his mother or his dad
And if that wasn't bad enough
He just lost the only love he ever had,

I said no one ever pleases everyone
When their life is done
You only have to believe in yourself
I believe in you, son,

I could see a smile in his eyes
As a tear rolled across his face
He thanked me for the advice
As he got up to leave the place,
Then he turned and said:

You're too young to be wasting time
Feeling sorry in your sorrows
Before you know it you've wasted years
And lost all of your tomorrows,
The only time you really have
Is the time you're wasting here
Life is out there for the living
Only broken dreams live in here.

THE VOYAGE OF THE MARIE-ALENA

The waves of the Emerald Ocean washed over the shore as the Wizard walked toward the village. Enyaw Nhoj had been watching him for several minutes. The ship was ready to sail, but not before the Wizard gave it a blessing. The wind was blowing from the west as Enyaw looked up at the two suns. The day was going to be a hot one. Hopefully the ocean breeze would keep the men cool. Tempers always flared easily with the rising of the temperature among the crew. Enyaw glanced back at the men of his ship. All were strong, able-bodied sailors. He wondered how many of them would be returning from this voyage.

"Hello, Captain." The Wizard greeted Enyaw upon reaching the dock.

"I was starting to think you had forgotten us." Not exactly a truth. Enyaw Nhoj knew the Wizard would keep his word. "Are you certain you won't join us?"

The Wizard let a smile cross his thin, beardless face. "I'll have to be much older than this before you can get me to go sailing upon the ocean. My feet prefer solid ground. Yet, I must admit I do envy you such an adventure as you have chosen to partake."

"To be honest with you, I figure our voyage will be more boring than anything else," Enyaw laughed heartily, motioning the other man aboard.

"This ship is more beautiful than I had imagined," the Wizard stated, walking up the gang-plank. "I trust she is ready for her maiden voyage?"

Indeed she was. Enyaw Nhoj had spent the better part of a year building his magnificent vessel. Only the best wood had been used, as well as the finest materials for the sails. Nothing had been left to chance. Enyaw was a perfectionist when it came to the ship that he was going to be the captain of. He had named her the 'Marie-Alena.'

"Tales of where you go paint a picture of great difficulty." The Wizard looked out across the waters. "Few have seen the other side of the Land of Elyk, but what has been told is that a rugged mountain range travels from top to bottom, with only a great cliff dropping into the sea."

"That is why I intend to find out if the stories are true," Enyaw grinned. "I have been to the north upon the Emerald Ocean and found no way to get around the Great Whirlpool. So now I shall go south. The passage to our furthest cape is calm. From there I shall learn what the other side of our land really looks like."

"I go with you in spirit. Take this with you." The Wizard held out his wooden cane.

A stunned look crossed the captain's face. "You have never been known to part with your cane. Some say it is magical."

"Take it!" Ordered the Wizard. "It may come in handy if you come across mystical creatures. The only magic it has is that which comes from the person who has it in their possession. The power will come from you. Trust in the cane and it shall guide you safely home."

Enyaw Nhoj took the cane, not knowing how to respond. The Wizard had trusted no one before with such a personal item. He was deeply honored.

"May this ship be blessed by all the Gods of the Heavens!" The Wizard shouted before turning and quickly departing the vessel. He never once looked back.

Enyaw Nhoj knew it was time to lift anchor and set sail. He ordered the six men of his crew to make ready. They would follow the coastline down along the western side of the Land of Elyk. With a little luck, they would reach the cape within a week. And so it was. As he'd predicted, the voyage south was calm and uneventful.

"We are near uncharted waters, Captain."

"Then we shall start charting them," Enyaw told his first mate.

Massive waves swelled as the ship made its way around the cape. Huge mountains came into sight as Enyaw spun the wheel, keeping his vessel within sight of the shore. The current was against them as waves crashed over the front of the ship. Judging the coastline to be uninhabitable because of the sheer cliffs that vanished into the roaring walls of water hitting them, Enyaw made the decision to sail farther out from land in the hope of finding calmer waters. He knew this would not be a popular choice among the crew. All sailing men knew to keep land in sight. Enyaw had broken the rule before and lost many a crew because of it. The time of men crossing oceans had yet to come. Only the daring ventured from the sight of land. Enyaw Nhoj was the first.

"Are you crazy, Captain?" The first mate asked.

"We have two choices as I see it. Be smashed by these great waves that push us toward the cliffs or find calmer water beyond the breaks."

"There is another choice, Captain. We could turn around and head home. There is no shame in the voyage we have already taken. We have seen the stories are true about our east coast being a vast range of mountains and cliffs."

An icy stare was the only answer given by the captain. This was his ship and he would sail her wherever he pleased. Nothing his crew could say was going to dissuade him from his objective. Enyaw Nhoj had vowed he would find the Sapphire Sea. He knew it was rumored to lie beyond the Islands of Hayeit and went all the way to the Land of Nodnarb. He would either prove or disprove their existence and all the legends that went with them.

"We never agreed to leave sight of land," the first mate yelled as waves continued washing over the front of the ship.

"All who make the choice to be sailors know that there can only be one Captain of the Ship. And as long as they are on said ship, the men are to do as the captain says. I am the Captain of the Marie-Alena. If anyone wishes to refuse my orders I will be pleased to let them off this ship the next time we reach land, if not before."

"Understood, Captain."

"Cheer up, mates. Don't forget we have the Wizard's cane." Enyaw laughed to himself at those words. How was a gnarled walking stick going to do them any good on a tumultuous ocean?

The Marie-Alena tore through the constant crash of waves as the Land of Elyk quickly disappeared from sight. It took the most part of a day before the waters finally became calm. The sailors were farther out than any had ever been. Nerves were on edge as each man stayed his post and wondered what their future would be. The only man on board who didn't seem to worry about it was the captain. He remained focused and in good spirits as three of the seven moons came into sight over the horizon. A blanket of stars would guide them through the night. As a slight breeze rustled through the sails, the men found themselves falling asleep after such an arduous day. Only Enyaw stayed awake through the night, never faltering from his course as he followed the northern stars.

"Land in sight!" Yelled one of the men, having awakened to the morning suns.

Enyaw smiled. "It is an Island. There are others to the east. Looks like a string of Islands, thus, the Islands of Hayeit. Get ready to feast your eyes upon the legendary Sapphire Sea."

There was a feeling of excitement as the men bustled about the ship. Breakfast was forgotten as the Marie-Alena glided by the first of many small Islands. An abundance of tropical fruits, the likes of which had never been seen before, seemed to pour forth from the forest. There was no sign of people. All of the Islands appeared accessible. It was time for the spoils of the voyage. Enyaw found a small cove and dropped anchor.

"Eat what you like, but only bring back plants with roots. If we can get some of them home alive, maybe the Keepers of the Land can plant them, allowing these new fruits to grow and supply sustenance for our people." Enyaw then had the small boat lowered.

The men spent the better part of the day gathering specimens to take home. When the last plant was placed below deck, Enyaw decided to allow the men one last luxury. They could return to the Island and sleep on solid ground if they wished. Only the captain remained aboard ship. He watched the men as they danced around a campfire near the beach. Where the others felt safest on dry land, Enyaw was more comfortable upon the ocean. He could not sleep unless he was rocking gently back and forth. The lapping of water against the side of the ship was his lullaby. And that night he slept.

The men were reluctant to leave such a paradise, but the yearning to return home had a greater pull among them. The only man with such an adventuresome thought was the captain. But he knew the men needed him to get them home safely. It was a duty he did not take lightly. Besides, Enyaw realized, they had yet to see the Sapphire Sea.

"Are we going home now?" Asked the first mate. "The storage rooms are filled to capacity with all the plants we gathered."

"There is one more thing we must do. Now that we know the Islands are real, don't you want to find the Sapphire Sea?"

There was no hesitation. "Yes, Captain. After yesterday, the men are with you all the way. Lead us onward to new glories."

It only took a few hours for the ship to wind its way through the Islands. As the Marie-Alena sailed around the last bit of land, the waters changed colors. The midday suns made the waves sparkle like diamonds upon a light blue sea. The men gasped at the entrancing beauty before them as the mesmerizing waters vanished into the far expanse. They could not tell where the sea ended and the sky began.

"This is the place of my dreams," Enyaw whispered.

"Do we continue on, Captain? Are we going to try to find the Land of Nodnarb?" The first mate queried.

"I have done what I set out to do," Enyaw began, "I now leave the decision in your hands. Do we go on or turn back for home?"

In unison the men agreed to continue their adventure.

"We will head north for two days. If we find nothing in that time then we will turn around and take our bounty back to our people." The captain knew his crew would like that idea.

The voyage went without incident the first day. There was nothing by calm seas and pleasant weather. The night brought only a light fog, allowing the stars to still be seen as they guided the ship. It wasn't until early the next day that a strange encounter occurred. Far on the horizon something popped up out of the water. At first, the men thought it was the mast of another ship, but soon they realized it had no sails and appeared to look more like a huge pole. As the Marie-Alena drew closer, the mysterious image sank back into the water. A few moments later the thing popped back up, much closer than before. The men could now clearly see that it wasn't a pole, but the long neck of a strange sea creature. The head turned, opened its mouth and let out a high-pitched sound.

"Grab the harpoons!" Enyaw yelled, turning the wheel of the ship furiously. "That sea monster is calling the others."

"What others?" One of the men asked.

Enyaw pointed ahead. At least six creatures were popping up and down on the horizon. "I'm turning around. We'll see if we can outrun them. If not, then make ready to fight."

The men quickly gathered the six harpoons they had brought on the slim chance of encountering a whale. The ship made a swift half circle as the creatures swam after it. The monsters had slim heads on necks about the width of a pine tree. They seemed to rise out of the water at a height close to twenty feet. The men realized what they could not see below the water was more than likely massive. Harpoons were made ready should the creatures attack the ship. Curiously, the monsters kept their distance, following at a steady pace.

"Could they be harmless?" Asked a sailor.

"Most unlikely. I think they are playing with us, hoping we let our guard down," the first mate answered.

Enyaw Nhoj had the same feeling. He swung the ship around again and headed west, knowing this would take them back toward the Land of Elyk and the strong southern current. His hope was to lose the sea monsters in the huge waves. He knew the Marie-Alena would do well as long as she was riding with the current and not against it. For the next several hours he kept a wary eye behind him, noting the monsters still following. A part of him wondered why they didn't attack, but at the same time he was thankful for that fact, because he doubted his men could fight off so many large creatures.

"Land ho!" Yelled the first mate.

The giant waves also came into sight as the captain sailed toward them. As soon as the mountains were clearly in view, the sea monsters made their move. Heads vanished beneath the water, but a wake could be seen as the creatures swam at great speed toward the ship. The men needed no instructions as they readied their harpoons.

"They breech!" Shouted the captain.

Four of the sea monsters shot up beside the ship. Harpoons sailed through the air, each meeting its mark, squarely through the center of the necks of each creature. The monsters screamed in agony as the weapons tore through their skin and ripped out the other side. They sank quickly into the swelling waves.

"Good work, men." Enyaw stated. "There are still three more and we only have two harpoons left. Make your shot count."

The ship bounced along swiftly as the big waves caught it in their grasp. The hope that the creatures would cease their chase upon reaching the southern current was soon dashed as the three remaining monsters rose up from the foaming sea. The two remaining harpoons found their mark, leaving only one creature alive. One very angry sea monster, having lost all its companions, dropped beneath the surface.

"We did it!" Sang out the crew.

"I wouldn't be so sure of yourselves just yet," Enyaw stated. "One still remains, even if we don't know where he is. I suspect the creature still follows us."

"Captain, what shall we do if it attacks? We have no more harpoons." The first mate had a wary look on his face.

"Take the wheel and head the ship directly for land. We'll turn hard just before reaching the cliffs. The rest of you men get below deck and make sure our cargo is safe."

"What are you going to do, Captain?" Inquired the first mate.

"Kill the beast when it returns."

The men did as told, leaving the captain and the first mate on deck. Enyaw pulled out the cane the Wizard had given him. If ever there was a need for magic, it was now he thought to himself. He moved to the front of the ship as it splashed over the great waves. The cliffs were near when the first mate turned the ship back south. Enyaw hoped the sea monster had left, but knew in his heart it was somewhere close. He didn't have long to wait before finding out he was correct. The monster lurched from the depths, hitting the ship with all its fury. Enyaw was thrown against the rails, but never lost his grasp on the cane. He quickly tied a rope to the magic stick. The last thing he needed was to lose what the Wizard had given him.

"Come on and get me!" He yelled angrily.

The monster was up to the challenge as it swam toward the front of the ship. An ancient evil shone in the creature's eyes as it once again vanished beneath the water. Enyaw knew what to expect as the monster suddenly shot up at great speed, exposing half its massive body. The monster was planning to crash down onto the ship and the defiant man. Enyaw threw the cane with all the power he had. The end of the walking stick sliced through the monster's skin, finding the heart. A scream of such anguish followed as the huge creature fell backwards. In a matter of seconds it was dead, floating on the waves.

Enyaw grabbed at the rope and pulled the beast alongside the ship. Once the men realized they were safe, they ventured forth and tied the monster securely. After Enyaw retrieved the Wizard's stick, the men knew it was time to cut up the beast and skin the hide. What shocked them all was the fact that the skin was so thick. They could not help but wonder how a mere stick had penetrated it. What none of them realized was that the cane was not made of ordinary wood, but from a tree of magic. The Wizard's walking stick had saved all their lives.

Enyaw Nhoj took the wheel of the Marie-Alena once again, so that the first mate could join in the celebration of their victory. He watched quietly as the crew told each other of how they had defeated the sea monsters, bragging more and more as the tale grew larger and larger. It was a story that would become legend through the ages. There would be songs sung of the voyage of the Marie-Alena and its brave captain and crew.

Giant waves moved the vessel swiftly as Enyaw laughed at the crew's antics. They were already acting out their heroic story, probably in preparation for when they would return home and share it with their families and friends. The southern current would take the ship quickly back to the cape and the familiar waters of the Emerald Ocean that they knew so well. A strange feeling of sadness came over the captain. He realized that once back home, the legend of their voyage would also be a curse. No sailor would want to return to a place with sea monsters. Enyaw also knew that he'd never have a crew again that did not make him promise to stay within sight of land before they'd sail with him. His big adventure would not likely ever be repeated. As the first stars of night appeared, Enyaw was reminded of the sparkling waters of the Sapphire Sea, and wondered if he would ever see them again. He then had to smile. At least he had seen it once. And his trusty ship, the Marie-Alena, had served him well. It was enough.

THE COMEBACK

Lady Luz had once been a pampered, much sought after actress of such exquisite beauty that Kings and Presidents basked in her glow. Of course that was thirty years ago when she had been the highest paid movie star of her day. Now she was rumored to be a relic of the past, basking in her former glories, ala' Gloria Swanson in 'Sunset Blvd.' It had been ten years since her last picture, and that had been one of the most famous fiascos in cinema history. She was now well beyond her prime at the age of seventy-two. Supposedly, bad investments and a worse choice of husbands had left her a recluse, clinging to the mansion her third husband had built for his Lady. Obviously a reminder of happier times. Millions had been offered to her in the past to come out of retirement, but she seemed to like the idea of being compared to Garbo and Dietrich, having thus far refused all offers. Into this world came Avery Shackleton.

The doorbell rang so loudly that it could easily be heard outside. Avery shuffled his weight from one foot to the other as he waited. This was more than his big chance. It was a last ditch effort to talk the reclusive star back into the limelight. If Avery could pull this off he knew it would put him in good with the studio heads. They would not only green-light his current film, but several of the others he had written and shopped around town. Not one to put the cart before the horse, Avery knew his future plans depended on convincing Lady Luz that she was right for the part. The only problem he actually saw with the plan was the fact that she wasn't. The script he had written called for a much younger woman, but that was why some of the higher-ups thought she might go for it. Vanity could be a strong bargaining chip.

The door opened and Avery found himself staring into the beautiful face that had not seemed to have aged for decades. He gasped at the realization that the woman barely looked older than him. And he was only forty. A sense of relief went through him as he stepped into the foyer of the mansion. She could easily pass for the age of his character after all, he thought to himself as the woman ushered him into a large room, filled with movie posters from her films.

"Please, forgive me for staring, but you are more breathtaking in person than I could have ever imagined," Avery stated eloquently.

The woman laughed. "I'm not Lady Luz. She is my mother. My name is Monica."

"Is someone here?" A small voice yelled out from nearby.

Only then did Avery notice the huge, throne of a chair at the end of the room. It was turned away from him, only allowing a view of a wrinkled hand on the armrest. He watched as his hostess motioned for him to follow her. The woman went around in front of the chair. "Mother, you have a visitor. It is Mr. Shackleton, the gentleman who wanted to talk with you about returning to the big screen."

By the way the woman was almost yelling it was apparent that Lady Luz was hard of hearing. "What is he waiting for? Tell him to come around here so I can see him."

The younger woman smiled at Avery as she waved him forward. He hesitantly stepped around the chair to find the legendary star. Once again his breath was taken away, but not for the same reason it had been before. The fact that Lady Luz looked her age was not the thing that caught him off guard. It was the way she was trying to hide her age under a ton of make-up and a hideous blond wig that sent chills down his spine. He could have dealt with a sweet little granny, but this grotesque caricature of a sexy starlet was nothing less than startling. Avery glanced at Monica, wondering why the daughter had not in some way tried to talk her mother out of such a freakish display.

"This is my mother, Lady Luz," Monica stated without the slightest hint of regret. "I'll be leaving the two of you to talk. Please let me know if you need anything. I'll be in the next room. Toodles."

What kind of phrase was that, Avery wondered? He still couldn't understand why the woman wasn't embarrassed for her mother. He gave a weak grin as Monica left the room and he found himself alone with a woman he could barely look at without wanting to bust into laughter. "So, Lady Luz, have you had a chance to read the script I sent you?"

"What?!" The woman grimaced her wrinkled face, which only made the powder and make-up flake off.

"I asked if you read the script," Avery hollered loudly.

"There is no need to scream at me, young man."

Avery was very apologetic. "I'm sorry, ma'am. I wasn't sure if you heard me."

"The story was good, but I noticed a few flaws. I don't have any bedroom scenes or a chance to show off the fact that I still have a very desirable body. Couldn't you write in a scene at a swimming pool?" A false eyelash was coming lose, but she hardly noticed as she fluttered her eyes at the man.

The urge to jump up and run out of the house as quickly as he could was something Avery knew he would have to fight. Instead he pulled out his car keys and fiddled with them in his hand. "I really don't think there would be any motivation for your character to be in that sort of position. She is a grandmother trying to get custody of her grandchildren."

"But all my admirers and fans want to see Lady Luz in a skimpy nighty. I won't do nudity, but it has always been expected of me to show a little skin."

This was not a conversation he had bargained for. "Those days are no longer here. I think your fan base would enjoy a more mature, graceful image at this stage of your career."

"Posh! I made my career on an hour-glass figure and these." She proceeded to grab her breasts and thrust them forward. It was not a pretty picture. "I would also need to have Bob Mackie doing my gowns. We need lots of sparkle."

"I think he's retired or dead," Avery groaned.

"Don't worry. He'll come out of retirement for me," she went on, ignoring the fact that he might not even be alive. "I insist on one of the Westmores to do my make-up and hair. Only the best will do."

Avery shook his head in disbelief. The only reason he even knew who the Westmore brothers were was because he had been such a movie buff growing up. These people she was spouting off were definitely dead and gone. "Let's not get ahead of ourselves here, Lady Luz. First things first. Does this mean you have decided to take the role?"

"With a big comeback like this, I wouldn't even consider refusal. Can't you picture the standing ovation as my peers finally bestow on me that elusive Oscar?"

The situation was funny. Lady Luz was already receiving an Academy Award for a film she had yet to make. How was Avery going to tell her the chances of that were slim when he couldn't even bring up the fact that her lipstick was smeared all over her face. "You do realize this would mean portraying a character a bit closer to your age?"

"I shall have no problem passing for a woman in her early forties. With the right lighting, we might even be able to say I'm in my late thirties." Not a hint of humor crossed the face of the famous actress. She was serious.

"I was thinking more in the range of late fifties," Avery suggested.

"Don't be absurd," Lady Luz laughed. "People would think I was an old lady. My public wants to see me as a glamour Queen. If I'm going to return, then my comeback has to be better than ever."

If only crawling under the table was an option. Avery was cringing at the thought of this Mae West impersonation doing his sweet, little drama. He had to wonder if the humiliation would kill his budding career. There was no way this woman was ever going to be able to act again. The studio, Lady Luz and he would all be the laughingstock of Hollywood. Now that he had actually met the woman, he knew she was better off staying retired. He placed his keys on the seat next to him. "I have to be honest with you, ma'am. My script might not be worthy of your great talent. As much as I hate to admit it, I think you deserve a much bigger showcase in which to make your return to the screen. Why don't we pass on this project and I'll write something especially for you."

A look of disappointment crossed the wrinkled clown face. "Are you sure about this? I dare say I was looking forward to acting again. Of course, you did say you would write a part just for me?"

"To show off all your wonderful talents," Avery lied through gritted teeth.

"I must concur with your idea. This project wasn't good

63

enough for me. You tell the studio I am passing on this one. I'll be awaiting the great role of my life, just as soon as you write it." She slowly got to her feet, putting her hand out for a kiss.

Standing up quickly, Avery gallantly took her hand and brushed his lips against it. "It has been an honor to meet you. I trust we shall meet again, sweet lady."

"Monica! The gentleman is ready for you to see him to the door." Lady Luz was all smiles, standing there in a dress that was two sizes too small. Avery was almost nauseous at the thought of her believing she was still the sexy young thing from forty years before.

"Did my mother agree to be in your film?" The true beauty asked, coming into the room. "She was so looking forward to a comeback."

Avery couldn't look the woman in the eyes, darting his glance to the floor. "She turned me down, but I feel it was in her own best interest. We have decided to wait until a project that is more suited for her talent pops up."

"Wasn't that sweet of Mr. Shackleton, my dear. So considerate of what would be in my best interest. I'm tired now so I think I'll go off to my room for a nap. Please, show our friend to the door." Lady Luz then headed for the hall at the opposite end of the room. Avery figured it led to the bedrooms of the house.

"I'm sorry this deal didn't work out for you," Monica said, leading the way to the front door. "Don't feel so bad. Many have come before you and failed as well. My mother seems set on staying retired. I feel she deserves it, don't you?"

"After meeting her, I couldn't agree with you more." It was not a surprise to him that no one had been able to get Lady Luz back on the silver screen. He had a feeling they had been like him and were thankful for her refusal. What would he have done had he not been able to talk her out of doing the film? It would have been such a disaster.

"At least now you can say you tried," Monica pointed out.

"If you don't mind my asking, would you have supported your mother's decision if she had decided to work again?"

A moment of apprehension crossed the pretty face. "To be honest with you. I don't think it would have ever happened. As I'm sure you noticed my mother suffers from a slight case of dementia. She has trouble with the fact that she is no longer a beauty queen. I play along because it makes her happy. Is that so wrong?"

"Not at all. So as not to ruin the illusion, I'll keep this on the hush-hush. I'll simply tell the studio Lady Luz wants to remain a mystery. Thank you for an interesting afternoon." Avery then turned and jauntily walked away from the home of one of Hollywood's most enigmatic stars. He was glad to at least know that the daughter was aware of the mother's odd tendencies to over-use the make-up.

It wasn't until he reached his car that he realized his keys weren't on him. Remembering where he left them, Avery knew he was going to have to go back to the mansion. At least he would not be running into Lady Luz since she had gone for a nap. The idea of seeing the daughter was not an unpleasant one. Under different circumstances, he might have even asked the beautiful woman out for a date. Monica probably had a full time job taking care of her crazy mother. As a film-maker, he had no time to waste on that sort of situation. Avery swiftly walked back to the house. A funny thought ran through his mind. What would Monica and Lady Luz think of his comeback?

He was about to ring the doorbell when the door swung open, a young maid he had not seen before stared at him. "I hate to bother you, but I was just here a few moments ago and seemed to have left my car keys in the study."

"Wait right here and I'll get them for you. Where were they exactly?"

"On the sofa across from the big chair," Avery directed. The young maid vanished from sight as the sound of women laughing echoed down the hall. Avery stepped into the doorway to better hear who it was. He knew at once it was Monica and her mother. What he didn't like was the conversation he was overhearing.

"Did you see the look on his face when he first laid eyes on me?" Lady Luz sounded quite coherent.

The maid returned with the keys. "Here you are, sir. Would that be all?"

Avery looked in the direction from which the laughter was coming. "Actually, Monica is expecting me. Don't bother to announce me, I want to surprise her. What room is she in exactly?"

The maid seemed flustered. "She is with her mother in the kitchen. It is the last door on the left. You can't miss it."

Avery strode down the hallway as if he had been there before. He knew a positive attitude and a good show would convince the maid not to bother following him. He made his way to the open doorway and stood in it imposingly. "I forgot my keys and didn't want to leave without saying once again how much I enjoyed the performance."

Lady Luz and Monica were both in shock as they looked up from the table they were sitting at and saw Avery. As he had suspected, Lady Luz was wearing no make-up at all and had also discarded the wig, revealing well groomed silver hair. She was also dressed more appropriately. It did not get by him that she looked very regal. This was the real Lady Luz.

"Please accept my apology. An old woman has to take what few pleasures she can when the time comes. Over the years I have learned that it is to my benefit to play a little game of charade with those who wish me to come out of retirement. This way they always leave feeling that it was their decision and not mine," Lady Luz explained.

"I feel like such an idiot!" Avery grinned. "You caught me, hook, line and sinker. I fell for the whole package. Did you notice how I was practically running out of this house?"

Monica smiled. "Join us and have a seat. We were about to enjoy some hot tea and muffins."

The look of a warm welcome from Lady Luz put Avery at ease as he sat down at the table. Then he had to wonder if it too, was also an act? "You obviously have not lost your timing. That was the best performance ever. Would you reconsider my film?"

Lady Luz shrugged. "Shouldn't a young fellow like you be out on the town with his wife? Stop wasting time trying to seduce old ladies."

Still not an answer. "I'm not married. What about the movie?"

Mother looked to daughter. "I won that bet. You owe me a dinner tomorrow night. Told you he wouldn't be working on so many different projects if he was in a relationship."

Monica blushed.

"What about the part?"

Lady Luz stood up exasperated. "Do I have to draw you a picture? I noticed the way you were staring at Monica. Ask my daughter out and then we'll talk."

Avery was learning it was useless to argue with Lady Luz. He turned to the beauty beside him. "Would you do me the honor of dinner tonight?"

"I'd be happy to be escorted by you," Monica smiled

radiantly. Avery had the feeling he was about to embark on the most important project of his life. Who cared about movies?

"What about our business?" Avery turned and asked Lady Luz.

The glimmer in the famous legend's eyes let him know this would be her final answer. "Don't ever mention again my comeback if you want to come back."

He never did.

THE BRIDGE

Thunder and lightning crashed through the night. Howard Stevens had been working late at the office as usual and lost all track of time. The midnight hour had struck as he headed the thirty miles home. There was little traffic on the highway as a thick shroud of fog rolled across the Ohio farmland. Howard chastised himself for not thinking to call his wife and let her know he'd be late again. He knew what her quick rebuke would be: "You are working too hard and are going to put yourself into an early grave if you don't stop and enjoy life more." What she didn't understand was the fact that they could barely stay afloat financially if he didn't put in all the extra hours. Running an independent Insurance Agency required a lot of hard work.

Bright lights appeared in the rearview mirror. Howard adjusted it to avert the blinding beams. He realized the other vehicle was approaching at great speed. It irritated him.

"What's the matter with this idiot? Can't he see how low the visibility is?" Howard spoke aloud.

A station wagon roared around Howard's car, pulling up alongside for a mere matter of moments before speeding off into the fog. What Howard had seen in the other car somehow disturbed him. A man and woman were in the front seat with the inside lights on and three children sat in the back, looking out their window. Their faces bore the look of such sorrow.

Howard sped up, wondering why he could no longer see the car's lights ahead of him. The station wagon seemed to have vanished into the fog. As he crossed the bridge over the river, Howard noticed that the fog had lifted and he could see for miles ahead. There were no vehicles on the highway in front of him. He wondered how the other car could have turned off the road so quickly without his noticing. A chill ran down his spine as the thought crossed his mind that they might have gone off the bridge.

"This is stupid," Howard said to himself. Yet, he had to know. He slowed down to find a spot to make a u-turn. "I'm sure they must have turned onto a side road." Though he was almost certain there were no such roads near the bridge.

It turned out to be no problem turning around and heading back to the bridge. The dense fog was thick as Howard drove slowly, inspecting for any damage to the railing on either side. There was none. A feeling of relief swept over him as he crossed the bridge and found a place to turn back around. Apparently, the other car had been going much faster than he thought and somehow sped out of sight. The station wagon had looked like a very old model, but it must have had a really good engine. Howard grinned. His newer model Chevy had been bested by an old jalopy.

The incident on the bridge never crossed Howard's mind again until a few months later when he was returning home from work late one night. Once again there was a thick fog as he approached the bridge. As before, bright lights blinded him in the rearview mirror and then the station wagon came into view and started to pass, but this time it pulled up alongside him and slowed down. Howard glanced over to see the exact same scene he had noticed before. Only this time, the children had their sad faces against the windows, looking at him. Never had Howard seen such anguished expressions. Then the man and woman turned in his direction. Howard quickly glanced away. The other car then sped off, vanishing into the fog. The feeling of deja-vu made Howard shudder. This time he didn't bother to check the bridge. All he wanted to do was get home and tell his wife what had happened.

For the next several weeks, Howard kept a wary eye out for the station wagon as he drove home from work, but there was no sign of it. He was almost ready to put it out of his mind when it finally appeared again. This time as it pulled up alongside him, Howard rolled down his windows, hoping to speak with the family. They only stared at him with haunted eyes.

"Do you need help?" Howard yelled.

The three children shook their heads up and down. The man and woman screamed in anguish as the station wagon roared away. Howard wasn't going to let them get away so easily this time. He floored the gas pedal as he took off after the other car. The fog was thicker than ever before. Howard realized there were no tail-lights in front of him as he crossed the bridge. They were gone.

More and more Howard found himself staying at work late during bad weather. It had become an obsession for him to find out why this family appeared so desperate. He'd even gone so far as to visit several of the local families in the vicinity of the bridge, hoping to find some information that would be helpful. But no one knew of a family living nearby with a vehicle that fit Howard's description. Even his wife was beginning to think he was taking things a bit too far. She couldn't understand why it mattered.

Over the next year, Howard saw the station wagon a total of seventeen times. Each incident was always the same, just before reaching the bridge; the station wagon came out of the fog, pulled up alongside Howard's car and then sped away, vanishing back into the fog somewhere on the bridge. The empty eyes of each member of the family seemed to be pleading with Howard for help. Somehow, he had made a connection with them. If only they would have stopped and spoken with him.

It was time to make a new game plan, Howard finally decided. Instead of driving home late during foggy weather, he would simply drive to the bridge and wait for them to pass there. Night after night he kept a silent vigil at the bridge, sometimes waiting for hours. His wife thought he was losing his mind, but he would show her. He was going to find that family and see where they went after crossing the bridge. After weeks of waiting and having no sign of the station wagon, Howard went back to his old ways, driving up and down the highway into the late hours of the night.

Howard had almost given up until the night the river flooded. He was a few miles from the bridge when the station wagon appeared and pulled up alongside him. He looked over to see the children motioning for him. The vehicle then pulled in front of him and drove at a normal speed. Howard was ecstatic as he followed closely behind. The fog and rain made it almost impossible to see, but Howard stayed directly behind the other car, surprised that it had not sped away as usual. An eerie feeling came across him as a flash of lightning filled the sky. The station wagon suddenly sped forward. Howard wasn't letting them get away this time. He gave his car all she had. There wasn't even time to hit the brakes as Howard realized the station wagon had stopped in front of him. Howard felt the full force of the impact as his car was crushed into a mangled ball of metal and hurled into the air. The splashing of water was the last thing Howard heard before sinking into the depths of darkness.

Abby Stevens was in shock as the officers told her of her husband's fatal accident. It appeared he had gone off the bridge into the swollen river. There had been no other cars involved, leading the police to believe he had been speeding and fallen asleep at the wheel. But the strange thing was, because the flooded river had swept his vehicle further downstream than it would have normally gone, the police had found another vehicle buried in the mud beneath Howard's. It was the station wagon of a family that had gone missing thirty years before. Their remains were still in the wagon.

It was months after the funeral before Abby could finally make herself drive the highway over the bridge. She hardly noticed the lights in her rearview mirror as a vehicle approached. It was not until the old station wagon pulled around her that she glanced over and gasped. It was the same family her husband had described to her so many times. But there was one difference. In the back seat sat Howard, looking out the window with the saddest expression she'd ever seen. The car then sped away into the fog.

BELOW BLUE ICE

There was no avoiding the situation. Selena was going to have to rappel down into the white abyss. If her theory was correct, this was where extinction began. She glanced at her fellow scientists and motioned them to join her at the fissure. It was going to take all of them to lower the equipment down into the depths of the glacier. The bulky, white contamination suits they wore would be no help either, she realized, watching the three men as they approached.

"Are you certain this is it?" One of the men asked.

Selena was sure. "I've gone over the data countless times. This is the place the plague first appeared."

"Hard to believe a place so beautiful could be so deadly," the man replied.

The irony of the situation had not been lost on Selena. She looked around at the majestic mountains of the Canadian Rockies. It was the most breath-taking place she had ever seen. The Edith Cavell Glacier had once been a favorite spot to hike among the many tourists of Jasper National Park. It was the journal of one such tourist that had brought them there now.

"We should lower one of you guys down first so that we

can make sure the equipment doesn't get banged up," Selena pointed out.

The three men went about the task of securing their ropes before one of them descended into the fissure. The remaining two men then slowly lowered the equipment down to him. Selena knew to stay out of their way and let them do what they were trained to do. She walked over to the edge of the glacier and looked down at the small lake below. Miniature icebergs floated to the far shore of the rocky bowl that had been carved out beneath the sheer cliffs of the mountain. A small creek ran down the valley, heading for the river a few miles away.

A slight breeze rocked the pine trees that rimmed the opposite hill. Selena found herself wondering what this place must have been like when birds and animals once existed. She turned around to see a second man vanish into the deep chasm of snow and ice. The glacier fascinated her. By all rights it should have already been gone. With the increase of global warming, most of the glacier fields had vanished. But for some unknown reason, this small, seemingly insignificant glacier still hung on in the shadows of the mountain which had nurtured it for centuries.

"Are you coming?" The remaining man hollered.

"I've waited too long for this to not," Selena smiled through her enclosed helmet.

She let the man slip the climbing gear on her as she nervously looked down into the nearby crevice. There was no sign of the other men or the bottom of the deep hole. A moment of fear crept through Selena as the man gave her the rope and told her to back herself over the edge. She took a deep breath and let herself fall back into nothingness. The training had paid off was her first thought as she rappelled down the side of the sheer, icy walls of radiant white. All fear was gone as an adrenaline rush took over and she found herself bouncing from place to place as she continued down. It only seemed like moments before she was at the bottom.

"That wasn't so bad, was it?" Asked one of the men.

"The first step was the worst. After that it was nothing but fun," Selena laughed as the two men helped her out of the ropes.

"So what are we looking for?" Asked the scientist.

A good question, Selena thought to herself as she looked around. She then pointed to a spot where the floor flattened out and widened. It was the most likely place to have another pit or fissure. The three of them slowly made their way, trying not to slip on the ice. Light radiated along the white walls in shimmering streaks as clouds drifted across the sun overhead. Selena found herself mesmerized by the glistening ice and snow.

"There is a small hole ahead." One of the men noted.

"If it is big enough for a person to climb down into, then it is the place," Selena replied.

The three of them slid down a small slope before coming to rest at an opening that went down at a ninety degree angle. It would easily hold a person and some of the gear. Selena made sure her hip pack was secured as she moved closer to the opening.

"This will be like going into a small cave. Should be no trouble. Do you want us to go first?"

No. I'll go in. I am the one who started this expedition. Besides, I'm the one who knows exactly what I'm looking for," Selena stated.

"You are finally about to prove your theory. What a find it will be to show that the plague was not an airborne disease."

Selena laughed. "I haven't found anything yet. There is

the big possibility we won't."

"Then let's find out."

Selena slid onto her butt and then very carefully worked her way into the snow tube. She found it easy to maneuver as she held to the rope and let the men drop her down to the bottom of the tunnel. A small room opened up to reveal what she was searching for. Blue ice radiated from the floor. There was ancient water flowing beneath.

"I found it," Selena hollered up. "It won't take me but a moment to get a sample and then you can pull me back up out of here."

"We aren't going anywhere." Was the response.

Selena cautiously crawled on her knees to a place where the blue ice was darkest. As she suspected, there was already a hole in it, allowing her access to the water below. She quickly opened her pack and pulled out several empty vials. In seconds she had her specimens of liquid blue. She carefully packed them back into the case before glancing around at the small ice room buried within the glacier. This was exactly as it had been described in the journal she'd read. The details of what happened were etched in Selena's mind.

The two young couples that had ventured onto the glacier and found the fissure would have had no way of knowing what they were about to unleash. They had climbed down and found the ice-room. Thinking glacier water would be the purest, they had filled their canteens before climbing back out. The woman keeping the journal had written her last entry after they had descended the glacier and stopped to rest at the lake. Apparently they had all drank the water from below blue ice and were starting to have stomach pains. Within minutes two of them had gone into convulsions and died. The remaining two, realizing they were sick from the water, poured it out into the nearby creek. The woman must have known she was dying as she scribbled what had happened very quickly. It was the last thing she wrote. She almost made it back to the parking area before succumbing. Her partner only out-distanced her by a few feet. A hiker found the bodies, took the journal and headed back into the town of Jasper to give it to the authorities, but it was already too late.

Within hours bodies started dropping all across Alberta, Canada. A few days later all of North America was a grave yard. It was almost a week before the plague hit Europe, spreading into Africa, Asia and the rest of the world. Nothing in its wake survived. Even the animals and birds were not immune this time. It wiped out every living creature. Experts had hypothesized that it had been airborne to spread so quickly.

Selena knew better. It had been in the ancient water, frozen for millions of years inside the glacier. She realized this had probably been what caused the extinction of the dinosaurs. She looked back down into the hole at the pure water below. Even with the naked eye she could make out the tiny creatures swimming about. A prehistoric parasite, locked away in the glacier until freed into the water system by four unknowing explorers. Once in the fresh water they had multiplied by the trillions and spread across the entire world.

"Haul me up!" Selena shouted at her awaiting comrades.

The climb out of the hole and then the fissure was uneventful as the scientists gathered up their equipment before making their way across the glacier. A beautiful sunset greeted them by the time they reached their aircraft. Selena looked out across the mountains one last time before following her crew inside.

"This calls for a celebration." One of the men grinned, taking off his helmet. "We finally have the answers to an age old question. What caused the extinction of man?"

Selena looked out the portal as the craft took off in flight. "But the real question is, could it happen to us?"

Little did she know that her world would soon be finding out. For once they returned to their planet, it would be discovered that the parasite they had brought back had not only brought about the plague through water, but it was also - airborne.

SWAMP WITCH

Abe Cutter did not like the mission his troop had embarked upon. He was a farm boy from Ohio wondering why he was suddenly in a God-forsaken swamp in the heart of Louisiana. As the four boats glided silently through the murky waters, Abe found himself watching Captain Johnson. The man's war record spoke for itself. Seven major campaigns, seven victories. Abe served the captain well, but he didn't actually care for the man. Most of the men were tired of the killing after four years of war, but the captain seemed to enjoy the violence. He was a sadistic, mean son-of-a-bitch.

A dense fog started to enshroud the cypress forest. It had been hours since they had seen solid ground. To Abe, this was a fool's errand. Their orders were to find and detain for questioning a rumored witch who had somehow cast a spell on General Grant. The only information they had been given was that this witch lived deep in the swamps. Abe doubted they could go much deeper.

"Sir. There appears to be an opening in the fog ahead. I

thought I saw a house," one of the soldiers hollered out.

"Quiet!" Captain Johnson pulled out his binoculars. "Ease up on the oars; we don't want them to hear the sound of splashing water."

The boats, each with five men, drifted with the slight current while the captain took stock of their situation. As the troops came closer, it was apparent that they had stumbled onto more than expected. A huge, three story plantation house appeared beyond the cloud of fog. How such a magnificent mansion could have been built so far into the swamp was a wonder. Yet, there it was, surrounded by cypress and pine trees covered in lush curtains of moss. There were no people in view as the four boats quietly pulled up to the shore in front of the house.

No instructions were needed for Abe to know what was expected of him. He quickly pulled up his rifle, as did the other men. With perfect precision, the soldiers disembarked the boats and made their way to the house. The captain stepped up onto the covered porch, motioning for his men to spread out.

"Hello! Is there anyone home?" Captain Johnson hollered.

The front door of the mansion swung open to reveal a large man, looking to be in his sixties, standing there in a red, silk robe. "What is this? Have I visitors?" A thick Irish accent was unmistakable.

"Are you armed, sir?" Captain Johnson demanded, pointing his gun at the man.

"There is no need for guns here," the big man grinned, noting the soldiers spread out across his front lawn. "I leave the politics to politicians and the war to you soldiers. I prefer to keep out of such things and have done very well by not choosing sides. As you can see, I have chosen a remote place to live, thus bothering no one and hopefully, not being bothered."

"Who are you? And where are your slaves and servants?" The captain asked.

"I am Seamus O'Flannigan. I own no man. As for my servants, all I employ is two black boys and a cook."

"How do you get your supplies?"

The Irishman looked amused at this line of questioning. "We have no need to leave this place. We live off the swamp. Everything I need is here."

"Bring out your help. I want to be sure you aren't lying."

A gun pointed at him seemed to subdue any argument. The big man simply nodded his head and two boys of fifteen or so came out onto the porch. Then the dark woman appeared. Her beauty was breathtaking as she smiled at the Irishman and then sashayed around the porch. There was defiance in her smile as she moved between her boss and the captain.

"What say you put down them guns and come in for some of my good cookin'," the woman said, her Cajun accent dripping with an earthy sexiness.

"I can assure you, there is no one else in the house," the Irishman stated. "If you would accept my hospitality, you are more than welcome to make yourselves at home. Eat with us and spend the night. Then tomorrow you can be about your business."

"Check the house," was the captain's curt reply, motioning for his men to do a thorough search of the premises.

Abe could tell the owner of the mansion was telling the truth, but he joined the others and checked out every room of the home. It was apparent that Seamus O'Flannigan had no lack of money. Artworks of exquisite beauty adorned the walls of the meticulously decorated mansion. It felt like walking through a museum. As expected, there was no one else in the house. The soldiers quickly gathered back out on the porch. The captain had never taken his gun off the four strangers before him.

"It's all clear, captain."

"Then we accept your southern hospitality," Captain Johnson smirked, "but do not be so bold as to think I will not shoot every one of you if I feel my men are in any danger."

Seamus grinned. "Their only danger is you. Be careful what is done in my home. As my guests, I would hope there is no longer a need for guns."

"My men shall remain armed. There will be guards on duty all around this house. We will accept your invitation to dinner. The men are hungry and could use a good meal. Is that acceptable?"

"Don't ask him," the woman swayed around her boss. "I is the one who has to cook for all these men. It will be at least an hour. Okay with that, captain?"

"Do what needs to be done, but don't try anything stupid. I'm sending a man with you to the kitchen to keep an eye on things."

The woman glanced around and then pointed to Abe. "I want that one. He can help me lift things."

The captain motioned Abe to go with the woman.

Once inside the kitchen, the woman wasted no time with small talk, but instead went straight away to the task at hand. Abe watched in amazement as she prepared a feast fit for kings. He did little to help, other than carry a big slab of meat from the table to a big cooking pot and she did let him slice the potatoes and carrots. Several times he thought about introducing himself and asking her name, but decided against it. By the time he helped her serve the food in the dining-room, the others had gathered around the table and were sitting quietly, as if afraid to speak. Abe noted four of the men were missing, no doubt guarding the outside.

"Did I not tell you my Lavidia could work miracles in the kitchen?" Seamus beamed with pride as the dark beauty went over and stood beside him. "There are those who have the magic touch. Lavidia comes by hers naturally. Her family practiced voodoo for years before finally coming around to my way of thinking."

A tense moment filled the room as Captain Johnson stood up. "Isn't voodoo a form of witchcraft?" His eyes demanded an answer from the woman.

"I do no longer practice the ways I was taught. It was a bad magic and made people go crazy. I am not the one you are looking for."

"Who told you what we were after?" The captain yelled, gazing toward Abe.

Seamus got to his feet. "Now stop all this nonsense. We are civilized people here. Let us just enjoy this delicious meal and talk about other things later. There is plenty of time for you to ask questions afterward, captain."

Abe could feel the tension as the two men stared each other down. Captain Johnson finally conceded the match with a laugh and sat back in his chair. The Irishman did the same. The two boys quickly poured water into glasses as the rest of the men dug hungrily into the food. It was the most delicious stew meat Abe had ever tasted. Once the men had eaten, they relieved the four outside, allowing them to come in and enjoy the meal as well.

"Shall we retire to the parlor?" Seamus finally asked, referring to the captain and those left at the table.

"Why not?"

Abe found himself sitting near the window as Lavidia lit

candles. Darkness was falling across the swamp. Abe realized he would not have liked to be out in it at night. The fertile farm country of home was missed more than he realized. He had to wonder why anyone would want to live in a bog of water and mud. Solid ground was much more to his liking. He watched as the thick fog rolled in around the house.

"How did you know what I was looking for?" Captain Johnson suddenly asked.

"Me know many things," Lavidia answered cryptically. "For instance, that boy don't like you very much." She pointed at Abe. "Neither do the rest of your men."

"This is war, not a popularity contest. I don't really give a damn what my men think of me as long as they obey my orders."

"They obey you. None of them told me why you was here. I know'd it the minute I saw you. That is why I tell you now that I am not who you are looking for. I set no spell on your precious general." Lavidia knew more than she should.

"You are the damn witch I seek!" Captain Johnson pulled his gun, and before anyone could protest, pulled the trigger.

The woman lay in a pool of blood as the stunned soldiers pulled their weapons. Seamus ignored them all, rushing to the side of his beautiful Lavidia. The big Irishman cradled her lifeless body in his arms. Abe could tell she was dead. He wanted nothing to do with this, but knew he was a part of it. They had come to find a witch. And now they had been the reason for her execution. He glanced at the captain for some understanding of the situation.

"What have you done?" Seamus roared with anger. "She told you that she was no witch."

"My orders were to find and kill the one who had placed a

curse on General Grant. I was only following orders," the captain stated icily, without the slightest bit of compassion or remorse in his voice.

"What happened, Master Flannigan?" One of the boys came running into the room, wielding a kitchen knife. Two of the soldiers shot him before there was time to answer.

Seamus was about to get up, an enraged expression on his face, when Abe hit him on the head with the butt of his rifle. The man slumped to the floor. Abe knew it had been the only way to keep the man from being shot. He looked around at the bloody mess they had made of the room. And for what? Because someone said a witch lived in the swamp. He was going to be sick.

"Find the other boy," the captain shouted.

"He's running into the swamp," a soldier pointed out the window.

"Don't let him get away! He could be going for help!" Came another shout. A second later was the sound of gunfire. "We got him," voices echoed from outside.

Abe ran out to the porch and threw up. He'd seen people killed before, but not for no reason. It was senseless to him that three people were now dead. In his mind, they didn't have to be. He was suddenly ashamed to be with these men. He no longer felt like a soldier, but a common murderer.

"I curse you. The lot of you will never escape this swamp." Seamus had obviously come to.

What Abe saw when he rushed back into the parlor was not to his liking. Captain Johnson and several soldiers were aiming their guns at the fallen man. It was an execution scene.

"Captain! He is unarmed. This isn't right," Abe yelled.

"So be it. Lock him in his room," the captain ordered. The men got the big man to his feet and hauled him away.

Abe saw the stern look on his commander's face. The captain stood over the dead woman, looking down at her flawless beauty. "My orders were clear. Once the witch was found she was to be dispatched by any means available. My course of action seemed the most expedient under our present circumstances. If I had allowed further discussion on the subject by the men, more than likely they would have insisted on taking her back for questioning. With that decision no longer in their hands, there is no reason for us to stay on here."

"You shouldn't have killed her," Abe whispered. "Or those boys."

"Sometimes we are forced to do things we don't want to for the greater good. That is the nature of war."

"Then I am done with it. I'm going home."

"No one deserts my command." The captain held his gun up.

An explosion ripped through the top floor of the mansion as screams came from above. Abe and Captain Johnson both turned to the open doorway to see a ball of fire rolling down the stairs. Forgetting they had been at odds, both men ran forward to see Seamus O'Flannigan coming through the flames. A soldier lifted his rifle to shoot the man, but was thrown back against the wall by some unseen force. Seamus raised his arms wildly into the air. Flashes of light and fire seemed to rain down around him. The captain lifted his gun, only to have it flung from his hand. Abe backed into the parlor as the Irishman came closer.

"What have you done to my men?" Captain Johnson bellowed.

"They are dead," Seamus stated. He then shot his fingers toward the two men, releasing pellets of ice.

Abe ducked behind the sofa for protection, but the captain

was caught by the full impact. It was as though he were being pummeled with hailstones. He fell to the floor as the strange display ceased. Seamus looked like a madman as he stepped over the body of the boy and moved to where Lavidia still lay. Abe watched all of this, afraid to breath. He knew the man's wrath was upon them.

"I was a most cordial host," Seamus yelled. "I invited you into my home and offered you food and drink. Yet, this is how you repay me." He picked up the woman's lifeless body in his arms. "Now my beautiful Lavidia is dead."

"I was ordered to kill the witch!" Captain Johnson sneered.

Seamus stood straight, with the woman still in his grasp. "Then you have failed miserably, captain. Lavidia was not a witch. But I am."

A look of shock crossed the captain's face.

"I gave you fair warning!" Seamus screamed, closing his eyes and murmuring some strange incantation.

The captain went for his gun, but it was too late. A burst of flame shot up through the floor and burned him alive. Abe fell back against the wall in horror, wondering what fate awaited him next. The Irishman ignored the only survivor's presence and proceeded out of the house, taking the body of his cook with him. Abe slowly stood and followed. Within a matter of moments the stately plantation home was in flames.

"Why have I been spared?" Abe worked up the courage to ask.

The answer was simple enough. "I'm going to need you to help me drag the bodies to the food cellar behind the house. Then you are going to help me rebuild my home from what is left of the ashes."

"Why did you put a spell on General Grant?"

"Because I wanted this war to go on indefinitely, but I

have failed. General Lee has surrendered. The war is over, boy."

"So you really are a witch?"

"In the old country there are those who believe as I, in the ancient ways of our Celtic forefathers. I prefer to call myself a warlock over a witch. It wasn't until I came to this country and met Lavidia and her family that I acquired a taste for other magic besides my own."

Abe grew silent as he slowly followed the Irishman to the wood doors that led down into a cellar. Throwing them open, he was shocked at the sight before him. By the light of the burning mansion, he could make out the two stacks of uniforms. One grey, the other blue. But more disturbing than that were the bones. Hundreds of human bones.

Seamus smiled as he dropped the woman's body down into the cellar. "Now you know why Lavidia's stew was so delicious."

MOON STATION SEVEN

Margaret felt a sense of uneasiness as the space shuttle landed. In what should have been one of her happiest moments, there was the impending thought of disaster. She let out a small sigh of relief as the shuttle docked with the station. Even though she had gone through this process a countless number of times, she always feared the worst until the green lights came on overhead, indicating that the shuttle was locked in and secure. Margaret had good reason to worry this time - her grandchildren were on board. She rushed down the corridor to meet them.

"Slow down, Darling. We don't need you falling and hurting yourself," Margaret's husband of forty-five years growled playfully. Chuck had not lost that youthful sparkle in his blue eyes as he glanced over at his wife.

"It's been three years since we last saw them. I can't help but be a little excited," Margaret laughed, "If only the kids could have come with them."

Chuck shook his head in agreement. "You know their work is important. They promised to make it up here by the year's end. Just be happy the grandkids wanted to come."

"I doubt it was about coming to see the grandparents. What teenager wouldn't want to visit the moon?" Margaret pointed out, glancing out the huge window of the station. The barren landscape seemed unending as it spread out toward distant mountains. The Earth was shining brightly in the starry sky.

"By the time they have spent a week up here, I'll bet they won't want to leave their wonderful grandmother." Chuck always knew how to say the right thing. Margaret put her arm around his waist as they walked toward the port of entry.

***

Amy felt such a relieve to be out of the claustrophobic quarters of the space shuttle. She smiled at her younger brother as they walked side by side toward the huge metal door. Amy was wondering how the reunion with her grandparents was going to play out, she had not seen them in years, though they had spoken several times on the radio at her parents lab. She was suddenly wishing that she and Todd were back home. Glancing at her brother, she realized that the thirteen-year old had no such misgivings. Todd had barely been able to contain his excitement when they had blasted off from earth. For him, this was the adventure of a lifetime. Amy wished she could have shared his enthusiasm, but she was very much like her parents. They had made it clear through the years that they preferred sticking on the good, solid soil of the earth. Amy had never understood how her grandparents could actually have lived on the moon for so many years without going crazy. Of course, she thought to herself, maybe they were nuts.

"Do you think grandpa will take me out for a walk on the moon?" Todd asked, nonchalantly.

"I don't know, but don't ask him. He's an old man and might not do that kind of stuff anymore. Let him decide what he wants to show you up here, I'm sure there will be plenty of things for us to do, besides, we are supposed to be here to visit with them." Although, Amy wondered what she'd have to talk about with her sixty-five year old grandmother. There was a fifty year age difference between them. She hoped her mother had been correct when she had said her grandmother was ageless.

"I bet grandpa will show me how everything works up here. Dad said he helped design all seven of the space stations. Grandma and him are supposed to be the foremost experts about the atmosphere and the geology of the moon." Todd loved showing off how much he knew, even though it was common knowledge back on Earth how famous their grandparents were. They were mentioned in every book about space travel.

"They are also retired. Did it ever occur to you that they might be sick of all that scientific stuff and just want to be left alone?" Amy posed the question to her brother. She also had to wonder why else they would have chosen to stay up on the moon instead of returning home.

Todd pushed the button next to the metal door. The sound of pressure being released through the walls hissed loudly as the door slid open. Amy found herself looking into the massive control room of Moon Station Seven. The grandparents were standing there to greet them. Amy was a bit surprised at how beautiful her grandmother still was. The woman's light, red hair, sprinkled with just a bit of gray, fell down around her face and across her shoulders. Amy realized how her mother and grandmother were often mistaken for sisters instead of mother and daughter. Her grandfather was still an imposing figure, standing straight and tall. The chiseled features of his face had not faded with the years. Even with totally white hair, he was a very handsome man, belying his Sixty-Eight years. The two of them could have easily passed for at least fifteen years younger.

***

Margaret held out her arms as the two grandchildren came through the doors. Todd immediately rushed forward and gave her a big hug. Amy seemed a bit hesitant, but finally did the same. Chuck embraced them all. Margaret was so happy to have Amy and Todd there. It had been a dream of hers for years to be able to show her grandchildren the moon, and now that time had finally come. She was so glad there had been no problems on the trip through space. The flights from the earth to the moon had not experienced an accident or mishap in over twenty years, but as history had shown with the Challenger and the Columbia, tragedy could happen at any moment. Margaret was not being pessimistic, just a realist.

"How was the flight?" Chuck asked, releasing everyone from his long arms.

"Awesome! None of my friends are going to believe I'm now an astronaut like my grandfather. Did you hear about me getting accepted into the Junior Space Program?" Todd beamed. Margaret realized he was exactly like Chuck, she knew they'd get along fine for the week.

"Of course I know about it," Chuck grinned, "who do you think pulled some strings to make sure there was someone to follow in my footsteps?"

Todd looked a bit shocked for a second. Margaret knew she'd better say something quick. "Don't listen to your grandfather. You got in on your own merits and we didn't even hear about it from your folks until after you got accepted because they didn't want this old buffoon to be disappointed if you didn't make it. Trust me when I tell you, this old man will try to take credit for everything if he can."

"Can I help it if the moon orbits around the earth because of me," Chuck laughed playfully as he punched Todd gently on the shoulder. By the grin that crossed her grandson's face, Margaret knew that he enjoyed being teased. That was good, because Chuck had always been a big kid at heart.

"Are you ready to head over to Moon Station Three? That happens to be where we live and it is going to take us a few hours to get there," Margaret stated.

"Hours?" Amy seemed incredulous. "It only took us a day to get here from the earth. Why would it take so long to get to another station?"

Margaret could tell that her granddaughter was at that impatient age. "Well, Amy, although we have made great strides in space travel, the vehicles here on the moon are fairly archaic. When your grandfather and I came up here ten years ago, we realized that balance and stability were a little more important than speed when it came to getting across the surface of the moon. The vehicles are old and slow, but they will get us to where we need to be safely. Besides, it will give us a chance to catch up without any distractions."

"Are you kidding!" Chuck bellowed, "It gives them a chance to see what the moon looks like up close. The kids aren't going to be wanting to talk once they look out those windows and see an entirely different world from their own."

"Can I walk on the surface?" Todd asked excitedly.

"Of course you can. I already had some suits sent over to Station Four so that we can all take some walks later in the week," Chuck pointed out.

"I hope you're not talking about me," Amy said, putting her hand to her chest. "There is no way I'm getting in a space suit to walk on the moon."

"Don't be ridiculous. Of course you are," Chuck shot back quickly. "This way you can go home and tell your mother that you have done something she hasn't."

"I've already done that by coming into space and visiting the moon," Amy concluded.

"Not meaning to interrupt this cozy moment, but we have plenty of time to figure out what the kids like to do once we get home," Margaret broke in, knowing full well that she was diffusing what could turn into an argument. In a matter of moments, she had noticed that Amy was exactly like her mother. Chuck had always bumped heads with their daughter in his attempt to push her to explore the unknown. He could never understand that some people didn't look at life the way he did. Their daughter had opted for a normal life on earth as a chemist, with a loving husband who shared the same passion and a family. Unlike Chuck, Margaret doubted her daughter and son-in-law would ever visit the moon. It had been a bit of a miracle that the kids had been allowed to come at all. Margaret knew she should count her blessings.

"We forgot to call the folks and let them know we arrived safely," Amy suddenly remembered. "Mom is probably worried to death."

"It's all been taken care of," Chuck assured his granddaughter, "The moment you landed safely and un-boarded from the shuttle, Captain Holloway radioed earth and let everyone know you were safe and sound. We'll talk to your folks in a few days from Station Four and you can tell them what a wonderful adventure this is and how they should be up here with you."

"I thought you said we were going to Moon Station Three?" Todd inquired.

"We are," Margaret replied, realizing the confusion of

talking about the different stations. "We live at Moon Station Three, but it doesn't have strong enough equipment to communicate with the earth. All of the Moon stations have different and unique purposes. Our nearest neighbor, Station Four, houses the communication network. Stations Two and One are basically labs for deciphering and experimenting with what has been found on the moon. Station Five and Six are where everyone lives while they are here. It's a lot like a luxury hotel, with different shops and restaurants in each one. I'm sure you already know what Moon Station Seven is for. This is where the shuttle and space pods land and leave from."

"So basically, it's an airport," Todd snickered.

"Why don't you live at Stations Six and Five with everybody else?" Amy asked.

Margaret glanced at Chuck. "We always knew we were going to want to stay here, even after our mission was over, so your grandfather built Station Three as our retirement home. We were allowed to stay on so that we could record the effects of space as we aged. Up here, the word retired doesn't mean much. Your grandfather and I still do geological experiments from our own personal lab."

"Don't you hate being so far away from everybody else?" Amy questioned.

"Not really. We happen to like each others company after all these years," Margaret tried to explain, "and we do get visitors on a regular basis because we are between the astronaut living quarters and the scientific labs."

"All the Stations are connected by one road and are pretty much in a straight line across the basin except for Station Four. It sits up on a mountain. That's why I had the space suits sent there. Just wait until you walk around up there and can see the horizon all around you. It's the most beautiful spot on the moon,"Chuck asserted.

Before Amy could protest, Margaret gave the girl another hug. "I'm so glad you came. We have so much to catch up on. I want you to tell me all about your friends and dare I ask, boyfriends?"

A faint blush crossed her face as Amy rolled her eyes. "Grandma! I just got here."

"You're right. There'll be plenty of time to talk after we get home. Besides, we still have a long walk to the other end of this Station. Your grandfather designed this place so that the land vehicles were far enough away from the space shuttles, so that if anything ever did happen, at either end of the station, it wouldn't impair a rescue effort." Margaret was proud of what her husband had accomplished.

"Pretty ingenuous, even if I do say so myself," Chuck smiled. If he only could keep his mouth shut, Margaret laughed to herself as they all started down the corridor toward the other end of Moon Station Seven.

***

Ann found herself looking up at the moon. It was so hard to believe that her parents and her children were on a space rock, orbiting the earth. A shudder went down her spine. The thought of hurling through the atmosphere had always made her sick to her stomach. The irony of being the only daughter of famous astronauts was not lost on her. As proud as she was of her parents, she knew there was no way she could have ever followed in their foot-steps. Luckily, Ann and her husband had cut out their own niche in the scientific world. They were a well respected team in the field of medical chemistry and had helped to wipe out several life-threatening diseases. Ann felt a bit guilty about the real reason she had let her children go to visit their grandparents. They would be bringing back several chemical compounds that could only be obtained from the moon. Her parents had been sending things back down to earth, but she knew they were hoping for her and her husband to come up and get some things for themselves. Ann knew her parents were anticipating she would fall in love with space and want to conduct experiments on the moon. It just wasn't going to happen, although Ann did know that there were certain compounds on the moon that she needed desperately for her own experiments. Sending the kids had been a way to appease her parents and make sure she would still get that which she needed, and besides, Todd had been dying to go. Even Amy had surprised her by agreeing to make the journey. After the kids had gone through six months of space training, Ann realized it was too late to change her mind and keep them from going. The one thing that gave her solace was the fact that she knew they were in good hands. Her parents would protect those kids with their lives and she knew it.

***

Amy hated admitting to herself that the ride across the surface of the moon had been more interesting than she had thought it would be. Todd and their grandfather had talked the entire trip. What had surprised Amy the most, was how it appeared to be night by looking at the sky, but there was enough radiant light reflecting from the earth to see everything for miles. Upon arriving at Moon Station Three, the four of them had disembarked from the land rover into an air chamber without ever needing to put on a suit. Once inside, Amy had noticed how comfortable and homey her grandparent's residence was. It seemed almost like a real house, if you could overlook the giant domed sky-lights that looked off into space.

"Are you kid's hungry?" Exactly what a grandmother

would ask. Amy smiled and shook her head back and forth.

"I am," Todd grinned as he flopped down on a large sofa and made himself at home. "Do you have pizza up here?"

Amy shot him a scolding look. "Todd will eat anything, Grandma. Just fix him whatever is easiest to make."

"We have pizza," their grandfather intoned in a serious voice, "But don't you dare ask for anchovies."

Todd started laughing. "No way!"

"What do you like, Amy?" She knew her grandmother was trying to make her feel at ease.

"Pizza is fine," Amy answered. "Are these fossils from here?" She picked up a rock from the shelf, noticed it was embedded with all sorts of tiny marks.

"Actually, yes," her grandfather answered, moving next to her. "At one time it was believed that life had never existed on the moon, but through years of study, we have come to realize there were once tiny, molecular creatures living just below the surface. The big mystery is what caused them all to become extinct?"

"Could it have happened when one of the meteorites hit? I noticed a lot of craters when we flew in from the earth," Todd pointed out.

"That is one theory. The only thing we know for certain is that nothing survived. There has been no sign of life on the moon since we first arrived in 1969."

"That is sure a long time ago," Todd cringed. "Too bad there aren't any strange space creatures for us to see."

"I can do just fine without meeting any aliens," Amy added, putting the rock back in its place.

"That is the one thing you don't have to worry about up here," her grandfather stated. "We've searched for years and found nothing. If life exists beyond the earth, it won't be found on the moon. It would have to come from elsewhere in space."

"At least there is one thing good about the moon." Amy turned to see her grandmother smiling. "There are minerals here like none on earth and your parents have put them to good use. Because of the moon, diseases like Leukemia and Parkinson's no longer exists."

Amy knew her grandmother was right. What her grandparents didn't know was that her parents were on the verge of another medical breakthrough. One of the compounds that would be going back to earth could very possibly hold the key to curing every form of cancer. Although she didn't always show it, Amy was very proud of her folks. It was cool to have famous astronauts in the family, but even that could never compare to being able to save millions of lives like her parents had done. The smell of fresh pizza brought Amy's thoughts back to the present. She actually was hungry.

***

The days were passing quickly, Margaret realized as she listened to Chuck in deep conversation with their grandchildren. The week was already half over. Margaret was so glad that Amy had finally loosened up and seemed to be enjoying herself. Todd had made it clear that he wished he could stay on the moon. That was something he'd have to argue over with his parents. It was so wonderful that the visit had turned out as well as it had. Chuck was in his element, showing the kids around the station and explaining all of the experiments that were done there. The four of them were about to venture forth on the biggest adventure yet. This was the day Chuck had planned a moon walk.

"Everybody to the Land Rover," Chuck demanded happily.

"Are you sure this is safe?" Amy was still hesitant, but

had changed her mind about donning a space suit and walking on the surface.

"Nothing is one-hundred percent safe," Chuck stated, "but this is no more dangerous than riding in a car. You should seize the opportunity and enjoy the moment. It will be magic."

Margaret had heard those words before. She hurried the kids in front of her as they went to the compression chamber. Luckily, Moon Station Four was only a fifteen minute drive. It was actually in view from their home, up on top of the nearby mountain. Chuck put his arm around her waist and smiled. Margaret couldn't help but love the man.

"Let's go show these kids some fun, Darling," Chuck said, giving her a quick kiss on the cheek.

***

Ann had been watching the moon through her telescope when she saw the meteorite shower. Streaks of light shot toward the surface with such speed that they were barely visible. She knew most of the space rocks disintegrated before they ever touched down, but it still gave her cause to worry about her children and parents. She hoped they would call soon. This was the day they had set up to communicate and she was feeling a bit uneasy. Ann knew that hearing her children's voices would be all she needed to calm herself. Glancing over at the radio, all she could do was wait.

***

"Wasn't that the most beautiful thing you ever saw?" Amy gushed from inside her space suit. "Those meteors sparked all sorts of colors as they came down." She was standing next to her grandmother. Todd and her grandfather were a bit higher up on the side of the hill.

"It looked like they hit over near Station One. We may have to go check it out. I hope Chuck saw what happened?"

"I'm sure he did, grandma," Amy laughed, pointing up at the others. The two males were jumping up and down excitedly.

"So, how do you like your moon walk?"

Amy had no words that could do it justice as she looked at her grandmother and smiled. "Thank you so much for talking me into this. I never dreamed it would be so cool. I'm finally able to understand why you and grandpa love it so much up here. If only mom and dad could see this, I'm sure they would love it too."

"It's the getting them here that will be the hard part. Neither one of them likes the idea of traveling in space. Maybe now that you and Todd have been here, you can convince them it's not so bad."

"They are probably like me," Amy admitted. "I was scared to death of getting in a space suit and leaving the safety of the Space Station or the Land Rover. Now that I've done it, I don't even remember what I was afraid of. This is so beautiful up here. Even walking without gravity has its appeal."

"You better be careful or you will end up like your brother and not want to leave," her grandmother pointed out. "Not that I would mind the two of you staying longer so we could get to know each other better."

"I'm so glad we came," Amy grinned, wanting to hug her grandmother, but knowing it was impossible in the bulky space suits.

"So am I."

***

Margaret was the first one inside Station Four, and therefore, the one to hear the communication board ringing, with all its lights blinking. Apparently, everyone on the moon was trying to contact them. She rushed over to the microphone and flipped the switch. Chuck and the kids were right behind her.

"Moon Station Four, this is Margaret. What's going on?"

"Did you happen to see the meteor shower? We think some of the remains hit the surface and our radar is showing signs of life!" It was the voice of Captain Holloway.

Chuck bent down, moving Margaret out of the way. "Are you sure? Couldn't the equipment have gotten messed up during the shower and sent mixed signals?" There was excitement in his voice. Margaret knew this was the moment Chuck had always dreamed of. For years he had insisted that life existed beyond the realm of the earth.

"We have positive readings coming from all Seven Stations. Something besides rocks came down with those meteorites. Teams are heading out as we speak from Stations One and Two for an investigation. Keep your fingers crossed. We may have the first contact with life from outer-space." Captain Holloway sounded confident. "I don't expect anything more than a bug, but I'd be happy with that."

Margaret leaned back over to speak. "Don't forget protocol. Something as small as a molecule could carry an unknown disease not known to us. Keep the search scientific and follow all the rules we've discussed should this ever have happened. We don't want anyone getting hurt because they are too excited and get reckless."

"It's too late to do anything about the excitement, but I will remind the scientist of how important this find could be," Holloway answered back. "Chuck, how soon can you get yourself over to Station Two? I know you are raring to go right now."

Chuck grinned at Margaret before speaking into the microphone. "I've got to get the kids back over to our place and then I'll head straight over."

103

"Can I go?" Todd asked.

"Not until we find out for certain that it is safe. There is also the chance that this all is a false alarm. Don't get your hopes up too high. If anything actually turns up, we'll decide what to do then," Margaret tried to explain. She knew by the way Todd rolled his eyes that it wasn't a good enough excuse for him. Not that it mattered, she wasn't letting him go.

Captain Holloway spoke again over the speakers. "I'm heading your way and should be there in a few hours, but before I forget, you have some other folks wanting to talk to their kids. Ann is awaiting your call on line three." There was a slight pause. "I'm not sure I'd mention what has happened up here until we have more details. We don't want to start a panic back on earth. I'll leave that to your discretion."

"We understand," Chuck replied, clicking off the switch.

Margaret knew her husband would tell their daughter. Despite the fact that they had always butted heads, he had always been honest with her and never kept secrets. She knew her daughter would remain calm and keep the news to herself. Ann had always been the one to analyze a problem before trying to figure it out and coming to a comprehensible conclusion. The only thing that worried Margaret was the fact that the kids were there in the middle of all this confusion. She knew that would also be foremost on her daughter's mind. Suddenly, she wished that Amy and Todd were back on earth, safe and sound.

Chuck flipped another button. "Annie, before I put the kids on to talk with you, there is something I believe you need to know…"

***

Ann held one hand to her heart, not realizing it was a habit Amy had unconsciously picked up from her. She could not stop thinking about the conversation with her parents and children. That had been hours ago, but it still weighed heavily on her mind. Her husband had told her not to worry and gone to bed. There was no way Ann could sleep. She kept finding herself looking up at the moon. It was only half there. Her thoughts were the same. What if something bad was going on upon that distant chunk of orbiting rock? There was no way she would be able to help her children if they needed her. She felt so helpless. For the first time in her life, Ann realized that she would have to trust that her children and her parents would be able to take care of themselves because she was no longer in control. A sense of guilt compelled her to go to the lab. She felt terrible that she had selfishly let the kids go into space to get a soil compound that she should have gone for herself. Not that it would have made any difference. If she had gone, the kids would have still been with her. But at least then, she would have been able to hold them in her arms and let them know how much she loved them. Ann felt a chill as the clouds covered the moon.

***

"Did mom sound a little weird to you?" Amy asked her brother as they both looked out the large window of their grandparent's home.

"She'll be fine. Dad said not to worry, chances of anything being able to live in the moon's atmosphere were slim to none," Todd tried to assure her.

"Dad did seem all right with everything. I can't believe he even told you to go check out the alien when it was safe."

Todd smiled. "I'll be the first kid from earth to see a creature from outer-space. Like to see anyone beat me out at show and tell."

Amy was glad her little brother could laugh at everything.

A knot the size of a fist was tying itself up in her stomach. She didn't know why, but she was scared. What if there really was an alien on the moon? Hadn't anyone in space ever been to the movies? Her grandparents were both giddy with excitement about the prospect of discovering a new life form. Amy felt like she was the only person on the moon who realized it might not be such a good thing to find.

"Would you like anything to drink?" Grandma was back in the room.

Amy tried to smile. "No thanks. Has Grandfather left yet?"

"After a long talk, we both decided it would be best for him to stay here with us and let the younger generation do their business. If they find anything, it will still be there for us to see later."

Grabbing at her chest, Amy rushed over and hugged her grandmother. "I'm so relieved to hear that. I feel so much better knowing he is staying here with us."

"I couldn't leave my girls unprotected." Grandfather was standing in the doorway, with a big grin on his face. "Don't look so worried. We have some of the best scientist in the world up here."

"I know I'm not going to fret about it," Todd smarted off, sitting back down in front of the game box he had been playing earlier.

"All of this will probably turn out to be nothing." Amy wished she could believe her grandmother's words, but she still felt apprehensive.

Before any more could be said about the subject, a loud buzzer sounded off. Amy had been at the station long enough to know that meant someone had arrived and was in the decompression chamber. She knew it was going to be one of the scientists with news about what was found.

Holding her breath, she watched as her grandfather turned and left the room. It was only seconds before he returned with Captain Holloway following close behind. A sigh of relief escaped her lips to see a familiar face. Todd jumped up from his seat upon seeing the pilot of the shuttle that had brought them from earth. The Captain had seemed to enjoy all the questions her talkative brother had thrown at him during their flight.

"Hope I'm not disturbing you folks," Captain Holloway stated with a smile.

Amy watched as her grandmother greeted the young Captain warmly. "You know that you are always welcome. Come on in here and have a seat. I'm sure you have a lot to tell us."

Grandfather could keep quiet no longer. "Don't keep us guessing. Did you find any signs of life?"

The Captain shook his head positively. "There was a small mass of living tissue at the crash sight. But don't get too excited just yet. By the time we got it back to Station One, all signs of life were gone. I suppose our atmosphere made it impossible for the thing to live." Todd gave Amy a look to emphasize what their father had already told them. She just ignored him as the Captain went on, "We ran all kinds of tests and found no type of disease or anything contagious. The scientist at Stations One and Two will probably be running tests for days. I'm taking a couple of tissue samples back with me for the rest of the teams at Stations Four and Five. I have a feeling no one will be sleeping tonight because of all the excitement about this find."

"You don't by chance think I could see what all the commotion's about?" Amy wondered why her grandfather had to ask that question.

The Captain grinned as he pulled a small vial out of his pocket. "I told you not to get too excited. The entire mass of tissue was no bigger than a button. I knew you and Margaret would want to do your own studies, so I got you a small piece of the puzzle to experiment on." He handed the vile to Chuck.

"Magnificent!" Other words popped into Amy's head. She was a bit disappointed at how small and insignificant this alien life form had been. It looked like a piece of thread. Watching her grandparents view the thing with such awe was way beyond her comprehension. For a person who had been frightened a few moments before, Amy now felt sort of let down. The entire incident was a dud in her eyes. At least she had gotten to see a good meteor shower.

***

Margaret knew she should have been with her grandchildren, but she couldn't tear herself away from the microscope in her lab. She had never seen such a complex group of atoms and molecules. Her and Chuck had been up all night looking at their latest acquisition. As excited as Chuck had been about the discovery of a new life form, Margaret was even more so. The only ones who had shown any disappointment were the kids. Margaret laughed to herself at Todd's description. They had been expecting a little green Martian and gotten something that reminded them of a splinter. She realized the kids would be awake soon and she hadn't started their breakfast.

"I think it's time to call it a night," she stated to Chuck. "Amy and Todd are only here for a few more days and we need to be visiting with them. This will wait until after they've gone."

"You are right, but it's going to be hard to not sneak in here," Chuck chuckled. "This is something I've dreamed of my entire life."

"Just be glad you lived long enough to see it," she consoled him, standing up and patting his cheek.

"I suppose I should take Todd and Amy back out on a moon walk since I cut it short yesterday because of the meteor shower. We'll head back up to Station Four after lunch, but in the meantime, you and I should take a nap and try to get a little sleep. What say we let the kids fend for themselves for breakfast?"

"Not a bad idea, darling." She wasn't above using his favorite expression. "I'll leave a note for Amy to let her know where everything is in the kitchen. If she doesn't want to cook anything, there's always cereal."

Chuck gave her a swift hug. "How did I ever find such a perfect woman? And beautiful as well."

Margaret laughed, "God knows you don't deserve me!"

Before she knew what was happening, Chuck swept her up in his arms and gave her a passionate kiss. There were no words needed for her to know how much he still loved and adored her. They had been together for over forty-five years and it still seemed as if it was only their honeymoon. Chuck was the love of her life. Margaret pulled away in mock indignation, looked her husband in the eyes and then pulled his lips back to hers. They were meant to be together, whether on the earth or on the moon. Their life was each other.

***

The second moon walk was as much fun as the first, Amy thought to herself as she watched her grandparents and brother bounce along the rim of the mountain. She hated admitting to the fact that she was seeing the appeal her brother had for wanting to be an astronaut. It was now on her mind as well, if only she had paid more attention to the space training she had gone through. Amy moved a little faster, not wanting to get too far behind the others. Her grandmother turned toward her and smiled. It was a smile she had grown to love. Amy was glad she had made the trip to the moon for more reasons than one. Even though the experience was exhilarating, it was getting to know her grandparents that meant the most to her.

"Mom has no idea what she is missing," Amy stated.

"Don't be so hard on your mother. This isn't for everyone. She hated space camp as a child and made it abundantly clear that if God wanted us to leave the earth, we would have all been born with spacesuits. As much as I want her to visit, I still don't think she would like it here."

Amy knew her grandmother was right. "No such problem with Todd." She pointed at her brother, who was doing somersaults in the air while her grandfather was bouncing up and down like a tennis ball. "Grandpa and he have certainly gotten close."

"As have you and I." A pat on the back from her grandmother was as close to a hug as a person could get in the bulky space suits. Amy knew this was one of the happiest moments of her life as she smiled at her grandmother.

The ground trembled. Amy tried to balance herself as another shock wave seemed to sweep across the surface of the moon. She wondered if it was an earthquake, almost immediately laughing to herself at the realization that it would technically be considered a moonquake. She looked to her grandmother for an answer. By the look on the other woman's face, she knew there was none. They grabbed each other and held tightly as another vibration swept the land beneath their feet. Amy glanced toward her brother to see her grandfather also holding onto him. They were both looking off in the distance. She turned the same direction. What she saw was not good. Moon Station Three was gone!

"What happened?" Amy whispered, looking to her grandmother for an explanation. "It looks like there was an explosion, but I didn't hear anything. Shouldn't there be fire and smoke?"

"Fire needs oxygen to burn. The moon's atmosphere instantly puts it out upon contact. The explosion was what we felt. There is no sound in space."

"Now, what do we do?" Amy was trying to keep from panicking.

"It's okay. We still have the rover. We need to get to the Station and contact the others to let them know what has happened." Her grandmother's calming voice was exactly what she needed to hear.

"Looks like it's time to move." Grandfather seemed totally unfazed by what had just happened. Especially in light of the fact that this was his home that no longer existed. He and Todd joined the two women.

"What about our stuff?" Todd asked.

"It's not there, stupid. Don't you realize the entire place has been destroyed?" Amy yelled.

"We don't have time to fight. Let's get to the Station so we can get out of these suits and figure out what happened," their grandfather said with authority. "I need you kids to act as mature as you can because we don't have time for childish squabbles. Can I count on you?"

Amy and Todd looked at each other and both nodded their heads in the positive. She had not meant to blow up at her brother, knowing none of this was his fault, but she was frightened. Amy quickly started down the hill toward Station Four. The ground trembled yet again.

***

"Chuck, thank God you're alive!" It was the voice of Captain Holloway over the radio. "All hell seems to be breaking loose. Apparently our little alien friend was only playing opossum. The scientist at Station One realized what they had was in a dormant state of existence, but when it contacted the same air we breath, it not only came back to life, it metamorphosed into a massive creature. All of the Moon Stations except for Seven and Four have been compromised."

This was not news Margaret wanted to hear. She looked at her trembling grandchildren before turning back to the radio. Chuck was keeping his composure as he spoke back into the microphone. "Station Three has been destroyed by some sort of explosion. We felt at least two other explosions while walking on the surface. What is the word from the other Stations?"

There was a slight pause. "Stations One and Two have met the same fate. No one got out alive. The fatalities are going to be astronomical. We haven't heard from Station Five. Station Six was able to get the creature out of the facility before anything happened there. They have it contained in a storage bunker close to the premises. I've sent word back to earth about what has happened up here. They are canceling all missions to the moon until the danger has passed. We have immediate orders to evacuate. How soon can you get here?"

"We are on our way," Chuck answered. "If I didn't have my grandkids with me, I'd swing by and check on Station Five, but I'm not taking any chances. We are coming straight to Station Seven."

"The shuttle won't leave until all survivors are accounted for. We'll see you when you get here." Captain Holloway signed off.

"What a disaster this has turned out to be," Margaret shook her head. "I don't even want to think about how many of our friends are dead."

Chuck grimaced at her, nodding toward the kids. "Then don't. We have a responsibility to get Amy and Todd back to their parents."

Margaret knew he was correct. There would be time to mourn their losses later. Right now, they needed to get to Moon Station Seven. A part of her wished the kids had not heard the truth, but she knew that even if they hadn't, Chuck would have told them anyway. He was a man who wanted people to know what they were up against. She had always admired that about him until now. Couldn't he see that Amy was scared to death? Despite herself, she knew he had done the right thing. The kids needed to know what had happened.

"We had best be on our way," Margaret tried to smile, as if it was no more important than a family outing. She knew if she stayed calm, Amy would do so as well. "Looks like we'll have to eat junk food at Station Seven for dinner."

"I doubt Todd will mind that," Chuck stated, grabbing the boy by the arm and pulling him up from his seat. Amy rose to her feet.

"What about the suits?" Margaret suddenly remembered.

Chuck gave her a loving glance. "We better bring them along, just in case we should need them. You get the kids in the rover and I'll bring along some extra supplies. No reason to not be prepared for anything."

Margaret knew what he meant, but dare not let herself think it. She only had one thought on her mind now. Get Amy and Todd to Moon Station Seven so they could send them home.

***

Ann was so pissed off at her husband. He had gone over

to the space center to find out what was happening and missed the call informing them of a problem on the moon. She knew he would be staying there once he found out. Because of the slim chance her folks might radio the lab, Ann was also well aware of the fact that she wouldn't be leaving for fear of missing their call. If only she had more information? All she knew was that there had been several explosions and fatalities at the Moon Stations. Nothing had been confirmed, but it had been inferred that this all had something to do with the alien life-form that had been found after the meteor shower. Captain Holloway had assured her that the kids were safe and on their way to the space shuttle. Her only comfort was the fact that they were with her parents. She put her hands over her heart and prayed all would turn out well.

***

The minute they arrived at Moon Station Seven, Margaret knew something was wrong. Emergency lights were blinking as they pulled the rover into the tunnel leading into the building. There was no sign of life. The four of them quickly got out of the vehicle. There was no time to lose. They had to reach the shuttle. Margaret just hoped it had not left without them. Even though she knew Captain Holloway had promised to wait, something could have happened to make it necessary for them to leave. From the looks of the place, it had been abandoned in a hurry. She noticed a half eaten sandwich on a table near the exit door. Chuck gave her a knowing glance. Words were not needed between them to know the urgency of their getting to the other side of the station. Margaret motioned the kids forward as her husband led the way.

"Where is everyone?" Todd asked.

"Let's hope they are waiting for us on the shuttle,"

Margaret answered. "We knew they would be evacuating the building," she added swiftly.

"But you would have thought a few people would have been waiting at this end to direct the survivors from the other stations as to what to do and to help if anyone was injured," Amy pointed out.

Margaret knew Amy was right, but she couldn't bring herself to say it. "Everyone from the other stations must already be here and accounted for."

"What if they didn't wait for us?" Amy gasped.

Chuck gave the thumbs up. "There are still the emergency space pods. If we have too, we can get out on them."

"But they only hold two people," Todd stated, "I remember that from space camp. Plus, they don't have enough fuel to reach the earth."

Why did they have to have such smart grandchildren? Margaret was well aware of the predicament they might be in. The space pods had only been designed for getting around the moon. They were never intended for travel back to the home planet. With a little bit of luck, there would be no need to worry about it. Hopefully, the shuttle had not left.

"Something is wrong." Chuck stood in front of the open cargo doors. "These are always closed. We better head back to the rover and grab those suits."

***

Ann grabbed the phone the moment it rang. The news wasn't good. Captain Holloway had sent a cryptic message back to earth. One of the scientists had broken protocol and brought a sample of the alien DNA to Moon Station Seven. It had decided to wake up and show itself aboard the shuttle. A creature of immense size was on the rampage when the message had abruptly ended. The only thing keeping Ann from breaking down was the fact that her children and parents had not been on the shuttle's passenger list. They could still be alive somewhere on the moon. She kept that thought in her mind as she hung up the phone.

It was time to do some analyzing of the facts. The chances of the space shuttle being flight worthy were now questionable. If the alien creature was still alive, it had probably done major damage to the ship. This meant the only other option would be the space pods. The main problem with them was the fact that they had such low fuel capacity. Ann grabbed one of her notebooks and started leafing through it. She was a bit surprised at her own calmness as she found what she was looking for. As long as her children were alive, they had a chance.

***

"What do you think the alien looks like?" It was the question Amy had hoped her brother wouldn't ask.

"From what we could determine from the cells we were studying, it would be similar to a squid. Of course, instead of water to live, it needs oxygen, the same as we do. That is why we went back for our suits." Her grandfather was pulling a cart with the bulky space gear.

Todd had another question as they walked through the empty space station. "Could one of them have gotten to here?"

"From what little we know, they cannot survive on the moon's surface. The only way for them to have gotten to any of the space stations was for us to bring them. Moon Station Seven should be safe. Captain Holloway told us there were no samples brought here or to Station Four."

"Then why are the emergency lights blinking?" Todd continued to inquire.

Amy was starting to realize that her younger brother was

more observant than she. "Todd, stop asking so many questions. Grandpa and grandma have enough to think about without you constantly quizzing them."

"It's all right, Amy. He's just asking out loud what we are all thinking," her grandmother stated. "Obviously, something has happened here and we have to assume the alien is in the building or the shuttle has gone without us."

Neither answer was the one Amy wanted to hear. "How will we get home?"

Her grandmother gave her a hug. "The space pods are in another wing of the station. They may be our only means of escape. We'll have to pair up and take two of them."

"But Todd said they don't have enough fuel to reach earth," Amy recalled.

"That is true, but they can buy us some time to figure out what to do. We don't have a lot of other choices if the shuttle is gone."

As they walked through the large corridors of the deserted station, Amy found herself peering into every shadow, afraid some slimy creature was going to be popping out of its hiding place. She wished the shuttle was closer as they reached the main terminal. At least there were no bodies strewn about the place. It gave her a bit more confidence to think that everyone was waiting for them on the shuttle. They continued their journey in silence. What only took a few minutes, seemed like a lifetime to Amy. At last, they were nearing their destination.

"Stop!" Grandfather's hand went up. "The doors to the control room have been left open. Let me check it out first." He let go of the cart and cautiously ventured into the massive room. He looked back and signaled for them to join him. Todd grabbed the cart.

"They may have left the doors open if they were trying to

get out in a hurry," Amy found herself saying as a certain amount of panic was setting in. "I don't want to go in there. Can't we just go back to Station Four and wait for a rescue ship to come?"

Her grandmother tried to calm her. "No shuttle will come here as long as there is the chance of an alien encounter. Our best bet is to leave the moon and go home. If it turns out there is no other way, we may still have to return to Station Four and figure out a plan of survival."

"It'll be okay, sis." Todd tried to smile.

Amy felt stupid for being frightened. So far they had seen nothing out of the ordinary, other than the station being empty and a few doors left open. More than likely, the others were all waiting for them on the shuttle. She swiftly walked into the control room. Her grandfather ran over to the radio system. She watched as he pressed a countless amount of buttons. A crackling sound came over the speakers. Voices became audible and Amy breathed a sigh of relief upon realizing they were in contact with the earth.

***

Pressing at her heart, Ann let out a deep breath. This was the call she had been praying for. She spoke into the phone. "Are you certain the shuttle cannot be used?"

Her father's voice sounded strong and confident. "Whatever was in the shuttle ripped the doors off to get out. I just got back from checking it. The inside was a disaster. Everyone is dead. It looks like they started a fire inside the shuttle to try and destroy the creature. We have no choice but to take the space pods."

"Are you sure they haven't been damaged?" Ann asked.

"We have no way of knowing until we get to them. Even then, I doubt they will do us much good. They only have enough fuel to get us half way home."

118

Ann looked down at her notebook. "Not necessarily. Were the mineral samples I asked to be sent back on the shuttle?"

"No. They should be in the cargo hold here at the station because we weren't sending them back until the kids left. Why?"

"I did a couple of experiments with the last samples you sent back and found that when it is mixed with sulphuric acid and then added to phosphorous fuel, it more than doubles the life of the fuel. I have the measurements all figured out and can give them to you now."

"This is one of those times when I am so proud of the fact that you didn't follow in our footsteps, honey. I hope you know how much your mother and I love you."

Ann didn't know what to say. "Here are the measurements..."

***

Chuck had just finished filling the tanks when Margaret heard a strange noise. She instinctively glanced over at the kids. They had heard it too. Something was moving around in the next room. She looked back over at Chuck. He didn't look happy. If only they could get into the space pods and leave. The thing that had not crossed their minds was the fact that the outer doors of the station could only be opened from the control room. Someone had to go back to switch the release. Margaret knew who it would be. Chuck wouldn't risk taking the kids.

"Get the suits on! I'm going to open the doors," Chuck ordered.

"Be careful," Margaret stated, "some sort of creature is out there wandering the halls. Make sure you come back to me."

Chuck gave her a big kiss. "Get the kids in the pods. I

promised I'd get them back home to their mother and nothing is going to stop me from keeping that promise."

Margaret watched as her husband vanished down the dark corridor. She turned to the kids. "You heard your grandfather. Put those suits on. We are going home." She started getting into her own suit as the kids did the same.

Todd snapped his helmet into place and then gave her the thumbs up exactly the way his grandfather would do. He then helped make sure his sister's was on correctly as well. Amy let a faint smile cross her lips. Margaret knew how scared she was, but so far, she had remained fairly calm. Putting her own helmet on, Margaret secured it tightly before looking back toward the dark corridor. She was trying to guess how long it would take Chuck to reach the control center and then get back.

"Something is in the ceiling!" Amy screamed. "I just saw some of the tiles moving. It's above us!"

The three of them rushed toward the corridor as tiles began falling from the roof. Margaret only glanced back for a split second to see long, black tentacles reaching down. As she left the room, she hit the button to shut the massive metal doors behind them. One of the tentacles shot out at surprising speed, grabbing Margaret by the leg. The door slammed shut, cutting the limb from the creature. The grip loosened as she pulled away from the broken appendage. Todd kicked it away. What Margaret saw next filled her with terror. The cut off limb was starting to grow. She realized that the alien was able to clone itself.

"Grandma, isn't this a decompression chamber?" Todd asked.

She knew what he was suggesting. "Yes. All we have to do is close off the air flow to these two rooms and it should kill the creatures."

"But how will we get back to the space pods?" Amy asked.

"We have air in our suits. Once the creatures are dead, we can go back in."

"I think we should hurry," Todd said, pointing to the creature growing in front of them on the floor.

They swiftly left the chamber and closed the doors. Margaret switched off the air. A shrill scream echoed through the silence. The three of them let out a collective sigh of relief moments before an explosion ripped through the building from the other end of the corridor. It had come from the direction of the control room. Margaret started running, with the kids close behind her. All she could think of was Chuck.

***

Amy was in tears upon reaching the control room. In the explosion, steel beams had come down and an entire wall had collapsed across the main controls. The smell of gas permeated the room. She could see her grandfather's crushed body beneath the rubble. He lifted his head and tried to grin. Blood was spattered inside his helmet. She knew at once that he was trapped beneath the steel girders. His injuries were massive. There was no way for them to get him out.

"That stupid creature ripped through the electrical box, causing a spark that set off the explosion. Now we know what happened at the other stations. It must be drawn to electricity. If it gets to the main power room, this entire place is going to blow." How her grandfather could still talk was beyond Amy.

"We've got to get you out from under all this." Her grandmother was pushing at the tons of twisted metal.

"There is no time. You have to get the children out of

here."

Amy leaned down next to her grandparents as Todd looked around. She somehow knew her brother was going to say something she wouldn't want to hear. "How are we going to open the doors to get back to the space pods if there is no electricity?"

Between gasps of labored breath, their grandfather answered, "We have back-up generators that will allow enough voltage to keep the station running for a few hours. There is a manual over-ride at each door. The biggest problem is that now we can't push a button to open the outside space doors and fly out of here."

"Isn't there another way to open them?" Amy asked.

Her grandmother held tightly to her husband before answering. "The only way to open the doors now is for one of us to stay behind and keep turning the switch."

Amy shook her head sideways. "No. There has to be another way."

"There isn't! We have no time to argue the point. You kids have got to get to those pods." The old man could barely stay conscious.

"Grandma has to fly the space pod," Todd realized. "I'll stay here with grandpa and open the doors."

Until that moment, Amy had never known how brave and selfless her little brother could be. She suddenly felt so ashamed of herself. "I can't leave you."

"Do as your brother tells you," her grandfather whispered, "You are running out of time. Go now."

Amy stood up and helped her grandmother to her feet. The older woman blew a kiss down to her husband. "I'm taking Todd with us to help open the doors. He'll be back shortly."

"I love you, grandpa," Amy cried.

***

Margaret could not believe they had reached the space pods without any problems. From what she could see, the pods had sustained no damage from the recent explosion. They were fueled up and ready to go. After a quick inspection, she turned to the kids and told them to get in.

"But I have to go back and open the door," Todd protested.

"Not this time, honey," Margaret told him, "I know you listened to all your training and made good grades at space camp. You have the ability to fly this pod. Take your sister home."

"Grandma, don't do this. Can't you take the other pod after the doors are open?" Amy pleaded.

This one time Margaret decided to lie. "I'll be right behind you kids. Now go!" Amy and Todd gave her a hug. "Tell your mother how much we love her."

She watched as they climbed into the small capsule and closed the hatch.

***

A sharp pain shot through Ann's stomach. She could do nothing to help her children but pray. The sun had recently set and she was just beginning to make out the shape of the moon in the twilight. For some odd reason she could stay in the house no longer. She stepped outside, letting the warm, summer air hit her face. Watching the moon had taken on a new meaning. Ann wanted her children home. She stared up at the orbiting sphere and prayed.

***

"Are you sure you can fly this thing?" Amy asked again.

"What choice do we have?" Todd answered. "Everything looks the same as the one I trained on at camp. I can do this."

Why hadn't she paid attention during their training for

123

coming to the moon? She knew they had explained how to use the emergency pods, but she had only learned enough to pass the written test and then proceeded to forget it all. Todd had insisted on taking a test flight. At the time she had made fun of him, but now she was glad that at least one of them would have some idea of what to do. Amy knew that if they made it back to earth in one piece, she would be seeing her brother in an entirely different light. He would not just be her baby brother, but also her hero.

"I'm turning on the engines so we will be ready when the doors open," Todd explained as he flipped the ignition. The pod fired up.

"This is so scary, Todd."

He looked at her and grinned. "We'll be okay."

***

Margaret tried to move some of the rubble away from her crippled husband. He tried to muster a smile as he spoke. "I knew you'd be back. Are the kids safe?"

"They are in one of the space pods," she replied, "what made you think I'd come back instead of Todd?"

Chuck gave her a knowing look. "You wouldn't leave one of your grandchildren behind. Besides, you didn't say goodbye. I knew you'd not leave me without that."

A tear rolled down Margaret's cheek. "You stubborn old man. I couldn't leave you here to die all alone."

"You better get that door open for the kids," Chuck pointed out.

Margaret hated leaving him again, but knew she needed to start turning the switch that would release the doors. She quickly went to the upper deck of the opposite wall. As she began the process, it gave her comfort to know that she could still see Chuck below. Impatience had never been one of her problems, but getting the doors open was taking longer than she had expected. After a few minutes she had it done.

"I'll be right down," she smiled at her injured husband.

"Stay there!" He yelled back.

Margaret screamed as the alien creature slid into the room. It was over ten feet tall. A massive black lump, with dozens of long tentacles. Within seconds it was upon her helpless husband. She watched in horror as the tentacles wrapped around him and began to squeeze.

"Kill the thing!" Chuck yelled angrily. "Cut the electric line!"

Margaret saw an axe hanging on the wall nearby. She grabbed it, planning to go down and hack away at the monster, but then realized what her husband wanted her to do. She knew where the gas and the main electric lines were. He wanted her to make sure no one else would have to encounter this beast again. She rushed over to the window and waited.

"Hurry!" Chuck gasped.

Margaret knew her husband would understand why she had to wait. She looked down at him as the creature continued to squeeze the life out of his body. "I will love you until the end of time."

The space pod shot off into the night sky, hurling its way toward earth. Margaret looked back at Chuck and knew that he had seen it too. Their grandchildren were on their way home. She took the axe and slammed it into the gas line. Glancing toward her husband one last time, she swung the axe toward the wiring, causing sparks to fly into the air. Margaret never felt the impact of the explosion as it ripped through the building. Moon Station Seven was no more.

THE TRIAL OF DOROTHY GALE

Upon her return to Oz, Dorothy Gale of Kansas was arrested and charged with the crime of murder. The Scarecrow immediately came to her aid as counsel. Bail was denied and Dorothy was cast into the jail at Emerald City. Because of only circumstantial evidence, her companion, Toto, was set free. The little dog went in search of the Tin Man and the Cowardly Lion, knowing they would be needed as witnesses for Dorothy's defense. The trial was set to begin on the first day of summer, giving the Scarecrow only a week to mount his case. What follows are the transcripts of the trial.

Bailiff - Please stand in the court. The honorable Judge Judy presiding.

Judge Judy - Everyone may be seated. I'd like to make myself perfectly clear before we begin, we are not going to waste a lot of time on this because I have an appearance on Regis and Kelly next week to plug my new book "Don't judge me or I'll throw your butt in jail."

Scarecrow - I couldn't agree with you more, judge. My client is innocent of all charges and this is a travesty of justice. The entire case should be dropped.

Judge Judy - Not so fast, bale of hay. These are some pretty serious charges. I can't dismiss the case just because your client looks all sweet and innocent.

Prosecuting Attorney, Frankie Morgan - I intend to prove that under all that gingham and calico lies the heart of a cold blooded murderer.

Scarecrow - I object! Dorothy shouldn't be judged by her clothes.

Judge Judy - Have the jury ignore that last statement. Now, gentlemen, I will not have any showy moments in this trial unless I'm the one doing it, understood?

Scarecrow - Of course.

Frankie Morgan - As you wish.

Judge Judy - Good! Now let's get on with this thing.

Scarecrow - I'd like to call my first witness, the Mayor of Munchkinland.

Bailiff - Do you swear to tell the whole truth and nothing but?

Mayor - I do.

Scarecrow - Were you not a witness when the Wicked Witch of the West threatened my client if she did not give her the Ruby Slippers?

Mayor - I saw the whole thing. The Witch made it clear that she didn't like Dorothy.

Frankie Morgan - Forgive the interruption your honor, but since when is not liking someone a crime punishable by murder?

Judge Judy - Good point. Straw-face better be bringing this around to some valid reason.

Scarecrow - I am simply showing that the Witch was threatening Dorothy. And it happened on more than one occasion. Dorothy was frightened for her life.

Judge Judy - Are there any more questions for this witness?

Frankie Morgan - I have only one. Were you not also a witness to the murder of the Wicked Witch of the East?

Mayor - Well, yes, but that was an accident. Dorothy didn't mean to drop her house on the Witch.

Judge Judy - Are you kidding me? She's killed more than one Witch?

Frankie Morgan - Yes, your honor. That is why I intend to show a habitual serial killer could be among us right here in this court. Who knows how many others she may have offed in her own land of Kansas? This girl is a danger to society.

Scarecrow - The other Witch was an accident.

Frankie Morgan - Were you a witness? I don't recall hearing that you were there. If so, please elaborate.

Scarecrow - Well, I wasn't actually there, but I have heard what happened from several of the Munchkins.

Frankie Morgan - Then let me call my next witness, the Leader of the Lollipop Guild.

Judge Judy - Let's dispense with the swearing in of every witness. They all know to tell the truth or I'll throw the book at them. Not mine of course, but it will be a big book.

Frankie Morgan - Give us your version of the murder.

Leader - It's like the mayor said, Dorothy's house fell on the Witch and she was pronounced dead by the doc. But the thing I noticed as the house was coming down, was that it was going in a circular motion, but at the last moment it dropped straight down onto the Witch of the East.

Frankie Morgan - And what would you believe accounted for this?

Leader - I saw Dorothy look out the window and grin seconds before the house crashed onto the Witch. It looked like a deliberate act of violence to me. Only after the Munchkins appeared did she show any remorse.

Dorothy - That's not true! I never saw the old bag until it was too late!

Judge Judy - Young lady, sit down and shut up! I will let you know when it's your turn to speak, so until then, keep it zipped.

Scarecrow - Could I call a recess until tomorrow? My two main witnesses have yet to be found.

Judge Judy - Are you pissing in the wind here, and then blowing it my way? I am the only one who gets to call a recess. If you have no more witnesses, the prosecution may proceed.

Frankie Morgan - Thank you, your honor. I'd like to call the Guardsman who gave Dorothy the Witch of the West's broom.

Judge Judy - It's about time we got around to the actual murder of the victim involved in this case.

Frankie Morgan - Did you see Dorothy Gale kill the Witch of the West?

Guardsman - Yes I did. And at least thirty other men saw the murder as well. Dorothy melted the Witch and then still wasn't satisfied. She wanted the broom.

Frankie Morgan - And why did you so willingly give it to her?

Guardsman - We were afraid of her. After all, she had just killed the Witch. She must have had some very powerful magic.

Scarecrow - I object! Dorothy has no magic, but the sweetness in her heart.

Frankie Morgan - Leading the jury, your honor. We want proof, not here-say.

Judge Judy - I agree. Crow's nest, one more outburst from you and I might decide to light a match myself. Next witness!

Frankie Morgan - I have no need to call all the guardsmen, you have their written statements. We have at least thirty witnesses that saw the actual murder. This seems like an open and shut case to me.

Tin Man (rushing into court) - Not so fast. I was there and saw things a little differently.

Cowardly Lion (holding Toto as he comes in) - And so did I.

Scarecrow - It's about time you two showed up. Where have you been?

Tin Man - We had a bit of trouble getting here. It seems that someone didn't want us to testify in this trial. We were passed out in the poppy field until Toto showed up, licking our faces to awaken us.

Frankie Morgan - Is this a trial or a reunion of fools? Can we get on with it?

Judge Judy - Exactly! Scarecrow, call your next witness. I can't wait to hear what will be said next.

Scarecrow - Thanks, your honor. I call the Tin Man. Tell us in your own words what really happened the night the Wicked Witch of the West died?

Tin Man - She wanted the Ruby Slippers from Dorothy and had threatened her life with an hour-glass. Dorothy only killed her in self defense.

Frankie Morgan - Were you actually present when said threat was made?

Tin Man - Well, no. We were still trying to get into the castle to rescue Dorothy. But I'm sure the threat was made.

Frankie Morgan - Of course. Dorothy told you so. We won't even mention the fact that you aren't a very reliable witness, especially after you just admitted you were breaking into the Witches castle uninvited. And I believe this was after you ignored the no trespassing signs in the haunted woods.

Tin Man - We had to get the Witches broom. The Wizard told us to.

Frankie Morgan - How convenient that the Wizard is no longer here. But the truth has come out. Dorothy was out to steal the Witches broom!

Dorothy - That's not true! I only wanted to go home!

Judge Judy - Shut up right now, young lady. Or you are

going to be in a world of hurt. Don't think for a minute that I can't see past those pigtails.

Scarecrow - How about my next witness, the Cowardly Lion.

Frankie Morgan - Please, continue on.

Scarecrow - Tell them how the Witch slapped you and tried to set me on fire.

Cowardly Lion - The Witch did strike me. And when she set the Scarecrow on fire is when Dorothy threw the water and melted her.

Frankie Morgan - Hold on a moment! Did you say the Witch set the Scarecrow here on fire? She was not doing anything to Dorothy at the moment that her life was so unexpectedly extinguished. I could rest my case on this testimony alone.

Judge Judy - Scarecrow, would you like try for a plea bargain?

Scarecrow - Never! Dorothy is innocent and I will prove it. I call Glenda, the Witch of the North.

(A bubble floats into the courtroom)
Glenda - Here I am. What do you wish?

Scarecrow - Please tell the court that Dorothy didn't murder anyone. She was only trying to get the broom for the Wizard.

Glenda - I cannot tell a lie. I have no idea what the Wizard asked of her. And I was not there when the Wicked Witch of the West was killed.

Frankie Morgan - But you did show up right after the Witch of the East was murdered. Was it not Dorothy who killed her?

Glenda - I suppose I would have to say yes. After all, her house was sitting right there on the crushed body.

Scarecrow - Don't let him twist your words. You know Dorothy would never hurt anyone.

Frankie Morgan - Sounds to me like someone's taken a roll in the hay. Could the Scarecrow possibly be in love with his client?

Scarecrow - That's preposterous! Judge, make him keep to the matter in front of us.

Judge Judy - I was sort of wondering the same thing, myself. I can't help but notice there is some straw in your client's hair.

Scarecrow - Can we please get back to the trial?

Judge Judy - Agreed.

Frankie Morgan - Tell us, Glenda. Why did you give the Ruby Slippers to Dorothy and not the next of kin, her sister?

Glenda - I knew they would be able to take the girl home. She should have stayed there.

Scarecrow - I have no choice but to call my client, Dorothy Gale.

Dorothy - Finally. I can tell my side of the story.

Scarecrow - So, do you have feelings for anyone here in Oz? Could that be the reason you came back?

Dorothy - What does this have to do with murder?

Scarecrow - Nothing, I just wanted to know where I stood.

Judge Judy - Me too. Answer the question, girl.

Dorothy - Of course not. I only came back to get some of those wonderful poppy seeds.

Frankie Morgan - As I suspected your honor. The girl is also a drug addict. I can't help but notice a life of crime seems to be the path this girl has been following.

Dorothy - I was following the yellow brick road, exactly like Glenda told me to.

Frankie Morgan - Do you do everything Glenda tells you?

Dorothy - Of course. She's the one who helped me leave Oz.

Scarecrow - Isn't she the one who showed up after you landed on your first Witch? And she gave you the Ruby Slippers. Then after the Wicked Witch of the West was killed she sent you home. Am I the only one noticing a pattern here?

Dorothy - And she is the one who told me not to take off the Ruby Slippers.

Frankie Morgan - Which would have solved all the problems in the first place. All the Witch wanted was her sister's shoes. Why didn't you simply take them off and give them to her?

Dorothy - Because Glenda told me not to.

Frankie Morgan - So you killed the Witch for a pair of shoes. How could such a tragedy have happened?

Scarecrow - I want to change Dorothy's plea to guilty without knowing it.

Judge Judy - There is no such plea.

Scarecrow - But there should be. Dorothy had no clue she was being misled the entire time of her journey. She has no magic. So how did her house come to land in Oz to begin with? It was brought here by someone else. A certain someone who wanted to get rid of the Witch of the East, but without casting any suspicion their own way.

Frankie Morgan - I am starting to see where this is going. Who would profit the most with two of the most powerful Witches out of the way?

Judge Judy - I know this one. It's Glenda!

Dorothy - But I trusted her so.

Judge Judy - Never trust in anyone but yourself.

Scarecrow - It was Glenda who sent Dorothy to the Wizard of Oz. A man who has long been rumored to be her lover. Together they concocted a plan to rid themselves of the Witch of the West. They used Dorothy to carry out their nefarious scheme with the promise they would send her home. Of course we all know Dorothy didn't make it into the balloon with the Wizard. If she had, I'm almost certain she would have met a grisly end by falling out from a great height. When this didn't happen, the Wizard skipped town under the suspicion that he and Glenda might be found out.

Glenda - It's true! It's all true. The Wizard left me to take the fall. But I found him. The Flying Monkeys did a fine job of making sure his body would never turn up again.

Dorothy - But I trusted you so. I thought you were my friend.

Glenda - Grow up, girl. You were the perfect patsy. All I had to do was make you think you were in danger from the Witch of the West and I knew you'd end up killing her. We didn't even need the broom. It was the big McGuffin to get you all worked up. Why didn't you stay in Kansas? We'd have gotten away with murder.

Dorothy - Have you ever been to Kansas? The minute I got home I was wondering why I ever left this place.

Scarecrow - Didn't you miss me too?

Dorothy - I'm sorry, but the Tin Man has my heart.

Frankie Morgan - Dear judge, charges should be filed against Glenda, but this in no way dismisses the charges against Dorothy. Misled or not, she is a murderer.

Judge Judy - I couldn't agree with you more. But let's let the jury decide.

And so it was that on the second day of summer in the Land of Oz, Dorothy Gale of Kansas was sentenced to life. Judge Judy in her infinite wisdom decided the best punishment would be to send Dorothy back home, never able to leave the state of Kansas again. Glenda was given a much worse fate. She was imprisoned in a bubble machine and forced to listen to big band champagne music for an eternity.

SOMEWHERE IN THE SHADOWS

The sound of a bubbling stream could be heard through the pines as Walter Cassidy made his way up the slight trace of a trail. His sister had told him it led to the remains of an old plantation that sat in a meadow, surrounded by the Blue Ridge Mountains of eastern North Carolina. Being a bit of a history buff, the idea of exploring what was left of a Civil War era homestead had been intriguing. What had especially piqued his interest was the story behind the place. Legend had it that when the wealthy Blaine family threw a party for their daughter's twenty-first birthday, a disgruntled neighbor used the opportunity to his own advantage by claiming the family were Yankee sympathizers and with a ramshackle group of Rebels, attacked and burned the plantation to the ground, but not before killing every living soul that attended the party. Needless to say, the entire community was shocked by the massacre and quickly rounded up the offenders and had them properly hanged. In the century and a half that had since passed, the story had become a part of the area's folklore. People had even claimed to hear the ghostly cries of the slain partygoers echoing through the valley. Walter didn't care about ghost, but he did like digging around old houses for historical artifacts.

"Now which way do I go?" he asked himself when the trail split off into two different directions. The right fork looked like it followed the stream and would more than likely end up in a meadow.

In all of his thirty years, Walter had never been one to take the most likely trail. He decided to see where the left fork led. From the looks of it, the trail went back up into a hollow, formed by the nearby stream. The sound of moving water was all he could hear as he made his way through the thick foliage. Obviously, the trail was little used. At times he wasn't even sure if he was still on it. Being an outdoors-man, he knew most trails followed the water-course. A small rumbling noise began to echo through the ever narrowing chasm as he picked out his way through the thick underbrush. Rounding a bend, Walter was astonished at what he saw. The small canyon ended at a hundred foot cliff. That which surprised him was the beautiful waterfall cascading down the rock wall. His sister and brother-in-law had mentioned nothing of this. One would have thought a visiting relative who loved to hike would have been told of such a find. He knew he was going to have to have a serious talk with his sister when he got back to her house.

Making his way up the wet boulders, he slipped a few times, but nothing was going to keep him from reaching the base of the falls. Large ferns and lush, green vegetation grew in the misty world that surrounded the scenic wonder before him. Walter found a dry tree stump to lean against as he sat upon the ground, able to look up at the roaring torrent of foaming liquid that catapulted down from the mountain. The sweet symphony made by the sounds of the water lulled Walter into a mood of tranquility. Before he knew it, he had fallen asleep.

The hoot of an owl awakened Walter from a peaceful rest. Darkness had fallen across the land. Beneath the canopy of tall trees, it was pitch black. Letting his eyes adjust, Walter could see that finding the trail back out of the narrow hollow would be nearly impossible at night without a flashlight. So much for always being prepared he thought to himself. He didn't even have his cell phone to call his sister and let her know he was okay. The one thing he did know was to stay put. No sense in hurting himself by trying to traipse out of the woods in the dark. He would stay there until the morning brought it's much needed light. His sister would probably never let him live this story down. The great explorer lost in the wilds of North Carolina. Walter settled himself back down against the log and listened to the melody of the night. Tree-frogs croaked in a comforting chorus. There was the occasional screech of an owl, probably wondering why this intruder was still at the falls. Walter had almost fallen back to sleep when something caught his eye.

A flicker of light shone through the trees. Walter sat up and watched as it moved in the distance. It was coming in the direction of the waterfall. He waited silently as the light grew stronger. The closer it got, the more he could see that it was a single light, probably held by one person. Figuring his sister had concluded he took the wrong trail, she had more than likely sent her husband out looking for him. He stood up, awaiting his rescuer.

"Am I glad to see you," Walter finally yelled out, trying to be heard over the water's gentle roar.

The person carrying the light stopped. Walter still couldn't make out who it was, but was fairly certain it wasn't his brother-in-law or sister. This person had seemed startled by his sudden presence. He hoped they still didn't have crazy moon-shiners in the hills. Could also be a teenager out for a midnight lark. The light began moving toward him again. As the mist swirled through the beckoning light, Walter could tell that it was a lantern. Droplets of water sparkled like diamonds as a woman stepped out of the shadows and showed herself. Radiantly beautiful barely described her. She sat the lantern down and unhooked the top button of her dark cloak. Pulling the hood down across her shoulders, long, auburn hair fell around her porcelain face. A faint smile appeared.

"I did not think anyone was here," the woman stated. "Are you lost?"

"As much as I hate to admit it, I fell asleep here at the falls and came ill prepared for the darkness. I thought you might have been my relatives looking for me. Please, forgive me if I frightened you."

"You can't scare me," the woman laughed. "These woods are my home. I was just surprised to see anyone here at this time of night. Forgive me for my bad manners, my name is Kathrina." Her thick, southern accent was soft and low. She offered her hand.

Shaking it gently, Walter kept wondering why she was there. "I'm Walter Cassidy. Very glad to meet you. What on earth would bring you up here in the middle of the night, if you don't mind my asking?"

He realized there was not a single blemish on the woman's face as she spoke. "This is where I come to meditate when I need to get away from the others. I like to think of this waterfall as my own special retreat. It brings me comfort to know that someone else feels the same way."

It was as though she could read his mind. "The minute I

saw this place, I knew it was special. Even more so now."
How corny could he sound? The woman didn't seem to
notice.

"I can guide you back down into the valley."

"That would be greatly appreciated. I hope I won't be
putting you out too much? You must have planned on
staying here longer than this?"

"It is all right. I found a better reason to be here. To
rescue you. Now don't think me a flirt, but it would be better
if you took my hand as we make our way through the forest."
Her smile was so inviting as he took her hand.

"If I stumble, I promise to let go and not take you down
with me," Walter chided.

"Just take it slow and we should have no problem." The
gorgeous lady then picked up the lantern.

The two of them walked in silence as they carefully made
their way down through the small corridor of light that
illuminated the path. Walter felt such warmth in the
woman's hand, that strange thoughts kept crossing his mind
as they walked. He felt like he was falling madly in love
with this mysterious stranger. Something in the way she
would occasionally squeeze his hand told him that she felt
the same. It was madness to have such musings. They
barely knew one another. Holding the lantern out in front of
them, Kathrina brought them out from beneath the covering
of trees. A bright, star lit sky shone down as Walter realized
they were at the fork in the trail.

"I guess I should have gone the other path. My original
intention was to find the old Blaine plantation. Of course if I
had, I would never have met you."

"Are you in a hurry to get home?"

"What do you have in mind, Miss Kathrina?"

She smiled, but with the hint of a blush that was

noticeable, even by the light of the lantern. "My family is celebrating the anniversary of the massacre. Would you like to join us?"

"Isn't it a bit late for a party?" Walter wondered out loud.

"Our friends celebrate the entire night. That was part of why I snuck away to go to the falls. There was no one there for me to dance with. Everyone already has a partner. If you're not too tired, come."

Oddly enough, Walter had never felt more awake. Obviously, he had slept for hours and was well rested. He was not a man to shirk away from an adventure. "Let me warn you. I'm not a very good dancer."

Kathrina seemed pleased as she pulled him down the trail that led away from his sister's home. They had not walked far before coming to a large clearing in the valley. A strange fog enshrouded them as they made their way toward more lights ahead. As they got closer, Walter could hear music playing. It sounded like a waltz. Such a haunting melody, wrapping itself around the entire meadow. When the fog began to clear, he could see a large plantation house, lit up with candles and lanterns hung all around. A band was playing near the house, while people in costume danced beneath the stars. It was the most mystical moment Walter had ever experienced.

"Can this be real?"

"There is magic in the mist tonight," Kathrina whispered. "For the first time in my life I feel like this was meant to be. Everything that has happened. Me finding you at the waterfall. You deciding to come back to meet my family. Could this be our destiny?"

"I don't know what it is, but let's enjoy it while we can." Walter took the lantern from her hand and put it down. He then leaned over to give her a kiss. Her embrace was warm and intoxicating as their lips met. Never in his life had he experienced a kiss such as that. He never wanted to let her go. For a man who had mocked the very idea of love at first sight, he was completely smitten. Never again would he scoff at such notions. In less than an hour he had fallen in love with the woman of his dreams. And he knew nothing about her other than her first name. The most perplexing thing was, he didn't care. She was his every thought.

"Let's join the others," Walter finally stated, picking up the lantern and leading her toward the brightly lit home.

"Can't we stay here, just the two of us," Kathrina pleaded softly. Her eyes sparkled.

"You were meant to dance." He twirled her around as they stepped into the crowd of people. Smiles greeted them as Walter sat the lantern down and swept Kathrina up in his arms. She didn't even seem to notice the others as they swayed to the music. For hours they danced, ignoring all who watched them. It was as though they were the only two people in the world as they waltzed across the ground, surrounded by a mist of fog, yet able to see the stars shining brightly down upon them. Holding the woman of his dreams in his arms, Walter prayed the night would never end.

As the first rays of a new dawn were streaking their way across the sky, an older gentleman walked over to the dancing couple and motioned for Walter to stop. The man then placed a small derringer on the ground. It seemed like such a strange thing to do that Walter looked to Kathrina for an answer. She seemed as puzzled as he.

The man then spoke. "With such a beautiful lady at your side, I felt you might need this in order to keep her there. Our time is almost at an end and it would be best if you began your journey home." He smiled and turned back toward the house.

Walter bent down and picked up the small gun. "What a strange custom. This looks to be very old."

Kathrina appeared disturbed by the gun he was holding. "Put it back. Guns frighten me. Please don't bring it with you." There was such sincerity in her voice that he could hardly refuse. He placed the gun back down on the ground.

"I should be heading back. My sister is probably worried to death about me. Will you be all right?" he asked.

She seemed puzzled. "I'll walk back with you. Perhaps I can introduce you to my family another time."

"I'm so sorry. I got so caught up in the dance that I forgot about everything else. When can we meet again?"

Kathrina smiled. "I'll be here tonight at twilight."

Walter gently kissed her before picking up the lantern and then starting back toward the trail. She put her arm around his waist, resting her head on his shoulder. They walked in silence, neither one wanting the moment when they knew they must part. At the fork of the trail they stopped. He knew she needed to get back to her family and he to his. He kissed her once more before handing her the lantern, turning and starting down the trail. Walter didn't dare look back, for fear of running to her like a fool. He had reached the cover of the trees when he finally glanced around. There was no one there. She was gone.

The day passed slowly. Walter had been able to wait no more and headed up the trail early. He was still furious with his sister and her husband. All afternoon they had argued with him about the Blaine plantation. He had seen the house himself and knew it to be in immaculate condition. They told him over and over that the house had burned down and all that was left was the foundation and two stone fireplaces. When he told them about the beautiful woman who had rescued him from the falls and all the people gathered together at the dance, they told him he was crazy. There was no house in the meadow. The closest neighbors lived clear at the other end of the valley. He knew they thought his imagination had run away with itself, but he also knew it had been real. His sister had even thought it might have been a dream, but Walter knew better. You can not hold and kiss a dream. Kathrina had been made of flesh and blood. He could still smell the lilac scent of her hair.

"I'll prove those idiots wrong," he laughed to himself upon reaching the fork. This time he knew to go right.

Long shadows were starting to fall as he reached the meadow. There was no question in his mind that this was the same clearing he had been to the night before. He started across it, wondering why he couldn't see the house yet. A knot welled up inside his stomach the minute he saw the ruins. Just like he had been told, there was a foundation with two large chimneys standing at each end. This had to be a mistake. Perhaps he had gone to the wrong house. After all, it had been dark and foggy. Then he saw something in the dirt. He went over and slowly bent down to study the item. It was the small derringer he had been given the previous evening. His heart sank. This was the right place. He picked up the gun and looked around. There were footprints in the dirt where he and Kathrina had danced. He saw no others.

The realization began to dawn on him. He had been among the ghosts of the Blaine plantation. That haunting melody from the night before would never leave his head. Nor his memory of the only woman he would ever love. Her perfect face, her soft voice, was already etched within his soul. He knew he did not want to live without her. Walter didn't know for sure what made him to do it, but he held the gun to his heart and pulled the trigger.

A gun shot rang out across the meadow. Walter staggered for a moment before falling to the ground, blood pouring from the wound in his chest. Who would have thought an antique gun would still be loaded? To his own surprise, there was no pain. He knew he was losing consciousness as the sun vanished over the horizon. It would be dark soon. He wondered if his love would be waiting for him. When she saw what he had done to be with her, would she be overjoyed? Would she be running to him with arms open wide? Life was ebbing away as he tried to keep his vision clear. Then he saw her. Walking across the meadow was the woman he would gladly die for. As the beating of his heart slowed, he felt such elation at the knowledge that he would soon be with the one who owned his dying love. Soon they would be together for all Eternity. The last image Walter Cassidy saw in this life was of a beautiful woman running toward him with outstretched arms. As promised, Kathrina had met him there at twilight.

***

The funeral had just been for close family and friends, but Kathrina could not help going. Even though she had only known the man for one magical night, they had shared such a special bond that she could not bare to not be there. She would always wonder what could have possessed a man with so much to live for to have taken his own life. Like a silly schoolgirl, she had envisioned the two of them sharing a life together. Now, it was to never be. A missed opportunity. She dabbed at the tears in her eyes. Somehow in her heart, she knew she would never love another as she had loved this stranger.

If only she had not allowed him to take the lantern and lead her to the old plantation ruins. They would have hiked on down the trail to the end of the valley and he could have

148

met her family and friends. Maybe then, things would have turned out differently. She had no idea why he had wanted for the two of them to dance alone under the stars all night long, but it had made her feel special in a way she had never felt before.

Why did he have to find that gun, she thought? When he first picked it up, it was as if he was listening to someone else in the darkness. She now wished she had taken it from him and tossed it into the brush. Who could have ever dreamed it would still work and that he would use it on himself? Such guilt would never leave her. Kathrina would always wonder if there was something she could have done to prevent such a tragedy. Years later she would hear that he had told his sister about a mystical party, lit with lanterns, where wondrous music played while people danced. Had Walter Cassidy seen ghosts that night that she was unaware of? If only she could have shared in the vision. The magic of the mist and the stars had been enough for her.

As the years passed, Kathrina always found herself drawn back to the falls. Because of the tragedy at the site of the old plantation, she avoided it like the plague. She never married, preferring instead the solitude of the forest. Her heart belonged to only one. And for her, that was enough. Since she had been the one to find Walter, his sister felt there was a connection between them and had become a good friend through the years. They never discussed Walter, but each knew that a bond had been built through him. It had brought much comfort to his sister that he had died in Kathrina's arms. What she never knew, was the fact that Kathrina was the beautiful lady from the story about the ghostly dance. She would keep that to herself until the day she died.

Forty years passed before Kathrina would again venture forth to the Blaine plantation. It was a hot summer night and she had planned on hiking to the falls to cool off in the mist of the hollow. With a flashlight in her hand, she made her way down the dark path. Upon reaching the meadow, she heard a strange sound. It sounded like violins. Then she saw the soft glow of lights coming from the direction of the ruins. She quickened her pace. The sight of the mansion, in all its splendor sent chills down her spine. People were dancing beneath the stars as a strange shroud of fog circled around them. This was what Walter had seen so many years before. She made her way into the light. A gentleman smiled at her, letting her know he was aware of her presence.

"You look as lovely as you did all those many years ago, ma'am. The one you are looking for is not here. He is waiting for you at that place in which you first met. It is time for you to meet him there again."

"Thank you," Kathrina cried, almost in a hushed whisper. She then turned and left the others in their perpetual splendor.

Kathrina's heart was pounding as she raced up through the trees. Age may have taken a toll on her body, but inside she was still that same love-struck girl of forty years before. The sound of the rushing water echoed all around her as she made her way through the darkened forest. At last, she could hear the roar of the falls and knew she was almost there. The soreness in her chest was getting stronger, but she didn't care anymore. Kathrina knew that Walter was there and they would be reunited soon. He was standing near the falls, waiting. She rushed into his arms and they danced, but their feet never touched the ground. They belonged to that other world. Now they would always be together, somewhere in the shadows.

INTO THE DUST

The streets of Cordova were deserted, except for one old man sitting in front of the hotel as the stranger came riding into town. He was a big, serious looking man as he rode the brown palomino. Dust was blowing all around as the stranger halted his horse across from the hotel, got off and tied the reins to the hitching post. There was the look of a gunfighter about the man as his pearl-handled colt 45, tied down low on his hip, was just visible from beneath his gray slicker. He turned and walked across the street, stepping up onto the hotel porch and addressing the old man.

"Do you know where I can find Billy Starrett?"

The old man glanced up at the stranger. Soft blue eyes peered from a wrinkled, but still handsome face. With silver-white hair, the old man looked like the perfect image of every kid's grandpa. "He's not here in this town. Billy Starrett was at Chimayo yesterday," answered the old man. His voice was graceful and sure, like that of a preacher.

"Have you heard when he'll be returning?" The stranger inquired.

"I can assure you, he won't be back this way."   He sounded like a man of learning and culture, out of place in this small New Mexico town. The stranger thanked the old man before walking into the hotel. After getting a room, he stepped back out onto the porch.

"Where can I get something to eat around here, old man?"

"If you want women and drink I'd advise the Cantina next door, but if you want a good, home-cooked meal, then I would recommend Megs Boarding House at the end of the street."

"Thanks," the stranger said, heading in the direction of Megs.

The stranger ate his meal slowly, glancing out the window ever so often. Megs was located at the end of the street and allowed a view of the entire town. The dust was still blowing hard. If not for the old man sitting on the hotel porch, the town looked abandoned. Occasionally, someone would come out of one building and walk swiftly to another before vanishing from sight again. The stranger was just finishing his meal when he saw a rider coming into town. He knew who the man was by the deep, jagged scar beneath the left eye. The stranger paid for his meal before stepping out of Megs and walking slowly down the street to where his horse stood. He started unpacking his gear as the rider rode up to the hotel.

"Where can a man get a drink?" The cowboy shouted, sliding off his horse. He swiftly stepped up onto the porch, staring at the old man.

"The Cantina is next door," was the whispered reply.

The cowboy was a big, brutish man. He moved closer to where the old man sat. "You look damn familiar. Have we met before?"

"We have not, I can assure you," was the polite response.

Angered at the way the old man seemed to be brushing him off, the cowboy grabbed the elder man by the collar. "I think you are a liar! There is something about you that seems really familiar. I damned sure know one thing for certain. I don't like you." He released the collar. "When I come out of that saloon, you better not be here, old man. Or I'm going to teach you some real manners." The big cowboy started laughing as he turned and headed toward the Cantina.

The stranger walked across the dusty street to where the old man sat. "Mister, I think you better take that fella's advice. He's a mean cuss and I've seen him shoot. He's fast with a gun and it wouldn't bother him to kill anyone."

The old man smiled up at the stranger. "You're a gunfighter too, aren't you?" he asked.

"Sometimes," the stranger answered, almost ashamed of his profession. The old man chuckled softly. It was odd, the stranger realized, with his being a gunman and telling someone how mean another gunman could be. He went into the hotel to unload his gear. When he came back out, the old man was still sitting there.

"Why are you looking for Billy Starrett?" Asked the old man.

"He's a gunfighter, just like me. I've heard he's one of the best. The man who outdraws him will make a nice reputation for himself."

"You do realize you would have to go up against his father if you were to kill him?" The old man pointed out.

A surprised look crossed the stranger's face. "Will Starrett! He was a legend with a gun, but I'm sure he's been dead for years. There is no worry about having to go up against him." He then started down the steps, turning back to the old man. "I'd really get out of sight if I was you. That fella' seems to mean business." He then walked back over to his horse for the rest of his gear and his rifle.

Dust was swirling in every direction as the big cowboy stepped out of the Cantina. The first thing he noticed was the old man still sitting on the porch. A look of venomous hate crossed his face. He stepped out into the center of the street. "I'm gonna' give you a chance, grandpa!" the cowboy yelled. "You are packing guns, so we are going to have a nice, fair shoot-out. That is, unless you want to run like a coward and get out of town?"

The old man stood up and put on his hat. He was a tall, thin man. Watching from across the street, the stranger slowly slid his rifle out and placed it across his saddle, aiming it toward the big cowboy. The old man stepped down from the porch.

"I hold no grudge against you, sir. So why do you wish trouble with me?" the old man asked.

"Because I don't like the way you was lookin' down your nose at me. I could tell you think you are better than the rest of us common folk. Let's see how good you are now?"

"I meant no disrespect. Can't we just let bygones be bygones?"

With a mean snarl, the cowboy spat, "You ain't backin' out of this, old man. There is something about you I don't like."

The stranger steadied his aim on the big cowboy as the two men in the street stood perfectly still, the dust blowing all around them. The cowboy suddenly went for his gun. Before he cleared leather, a bullet ripped through his chest, knocking him backwards into the dirt. The stranger stood in complete shock. He never even had a chance to fire his rifle. He turned to see the old man holstering his gun. The street was silent, except for the sound of the wind blowing.

"Thanks," the old man stated, turning toward the stranger.

He then walked to the stable. A few minutes later he came riding out on a large, black stallion. He rode slowly and proudly down the dusty street. Once again, he tipped his hat to the stranger as he rode past.

Some men came running out of the Cantina and stood around the body of the dead cowboy. As a crowd gathered, the stranger walked over to the hotel and then turned to watch as the old man disappeared into the dusty landscape. He then heard one of the men telling the others that Billy Starrett had been killed the day before by the big, scar faced gunman in Chimayo. The stranger smiled as he looked one last time toward the dust cloud that was leaving town.

THE BILLY BOY BANJO BAND

Lisette had not seen the man of her dreams for over fifty years. Yet, he was always in her thoughts. Their brief romance, a long ago memory that had sustained her through the decades. She had never married, knowing that no man could replace the love of her life in her heart. A heart that had skipped a beat when she saw the flyer in the local paper. 'The Billy Boy Banjo Band' was going to be appearing at the gazebo in the nearby park. One of those nostalgic gatherings for the residents of a small town to remember what once was. Lisette had a better reason to attend. The leader of the band was her lost love.

It had been the summer of 1959 when Lisette and some friends from school had snuck out of their houses and gone to the local dancing establishment. Because the band had struck a chord with the youth of the Midwest it had become quite popular. Especially the bandleader, a strapping young man with a charismatic personality. Billy Boy loved the ladies. And they loved him. Lisette had taken one look and knew Billy was out of her league. She fell in love anyway.

The band played a varied selection of tunes, ranging from country swing to folk to pop. Billy Boy played the banjo with magic fingers. There was no doubting his talent. He was a rising star. Lisette went night after night to listen to the music. Her devotion had apparently caught the bandleader's attention. He finally went down to the dance floor and made her introduce herself to him. They danced and laughed for a few songs before he returned to the stage, but not without getting a promise from her that she'd wait for him after the show.

Lisette and Billy Boy were inseparable after that. The band signed on to stay for two months. A seventeen year old girl and her twenty-two year old love walked hand in hand beneath the stars of one memorable summer. But like all good things, the summer came to an end.

Billy Boy and his band were ready to hit the open road. Fame and fortune awaited them elsewhere. As Billy had said, there was no future in small towns. Lisette would have been willing to go if she'd been asked, but there was no invitation. Billy did say he'd be back to marry her someday. He vowed his undying love as they parted. That was the last she ever heard from him.

A big red hat and scarf from her club put the finishing touch on Lisette's outfit. She was sitting in a lawn chair, watching the townspeople gather in the park for the concert. It was a perfect October day. No wind, mild temperatures. Smiling faces greeted her as friends and neighbors waved. The small town life Billy Boy had so rejected had turned out to be a good life for Lisette. She had started with giving piano lessons before opening a music store in town. A store she was proud to say was still open after forty years. Lisette had few regrets.

A slight breeze rocked the willows near the gazebo as the band finally made their way up. Four old men lifted instruments as a fifth man came forward and smiled at the fifty or so people in the park. Lisette knew immediately that it was Billy Boy, despite the receding white hair and the heavy paunch. He still had the old swagger as he winked at some of the ladies. The banjo then came up and it was nice to hear that he had not lost the magic. For more than an hour the band played a sweet collection of folk and old ballads. A fitting selection to recall the nostalgia of days gone by.

A singing group from the local school was next. The real reason so many had shown up. Lisette watched as Billy and the band moved over to some tables to sell their CD's. She was a bit apprehensive as she approached. Billy looked her way and smiled. The smile of a stranger.

"Did you enjoy our music?" Billy asked.

"It made for a lovely evening," Lisette answered. "Do you do many shows like this?"

Billy grinned, "More than I wish. We travel all over the country looking for our next gig. Most of them now seem to be at Senior Centers or fairs. Believe it or not, but we once had a top-forty hit back in the early sixties."

"I have the album."

A surprised look crossed the man's face. "Have we met before?"

Lisette smiled. "Don't you remember?"

"Of course," Billy lied. "It was down in Austin, or was it San Antonio?"

Laughing, Lisette touched his arm. "I take it you've been with many women through the years. I've seldom left this town. Does that help any?"

Billy turned to the guys. "I told you I thought we'd been here before. This is the town we stayed the summer back in '59."

"But do you remember the name of the girl you promised to come back and marry?" Lisette asked.

"My God, is it really you. Lisette!"

So he had remembered her name after all the years. Lisette gave him a big hug as he came from around the table. He took her by the arm and led her beneath one of the willow trees. There was so much she wanted to ask him. To tell him. But from the moment he realized who she was, he never stopped talking. She learned he'd been married three times. Of course none of his wives had ever understood that with his band he had to be away from home most of the time. He'd had a drinking problem, but had finally wrestled that demon down. The band had broken up several times over the years, yet always managed to get back together when times got hard.

Lisette finally broke in. "Have you been happy, Billy Boy? Was life on the road all that you thought it would be?"

The man glanced away, watching the young people on the stage as they sang. "I made one big mistake in my life. That was not staying here with you. I've regretted that decision every day since I left. I never did become the big success I thought I would be. So now I ask myself what might have been if I'd settled down in a town like this with someone like you?"

"You'd have been miserable," Lisette smiled. "And I believe you are still the same old charmer you always were, telling people what they want to hear. Nothing kept you from coming back. I've always been here."

Billy frowned. "What do you mean by that? I have come back."

159

"But not for me. You'd forgotten all about this town. Our meeting is merely a sweet accident."

Letting out a sigh of relief, Billy inquired, "How long did you wait for me to return before you finally decided to get married?"

"I never married. You truly were my first love."

"I'm so sorry I was such an ass. I figured after a few weeks you'd realize we were simply a summer fling. I've been with countless women since that time and made many similar promises. Only now the pickings are far and few for an old fat man with a banjo."

"But you never really answered my question. Have you been happy?"

"Yes. Even in these old bones, the call of the open road still calls to me. I was born to be in a traveling band. It's the only life I really know."

"That was all I needed to hear," Lisette stated. "I want you to know that my life has been wonderful, just from loving you those few months a lifetime ago. Perhaps we'll meet again if you ever happen back to this town." She then turned and walked out of Billy Boy's life, knowing it would be forever.

Lisette saw the car pull up to the curb as a handsome man of forty-nine stepped out. She was never more radiantly beautiful than in that moment as she took her son's hand and got into the vehicle. Billy may have been her first love, but their son had been her greatest.

THE DARKNESS BENEATH

What should have been a simple day of spelunking had turned into a nightmare. Andy was as much to blame as anyone. If they had only stuck to the original plan, but no, he had to suggest a more challenging adventure. The minute he mentioned skipping the cave they had told everyone they were going to and tackling one with some technical climbs, he had his companion's rapt attention. Now here they were, seventeen miles from where they should have been, and several hours underground. Needless to say, nothing had gone right from the moment they made their descent into the small pit opening. Maggie was the first to suffer injury when her rope slipped, dropping her about fifteen feet. She hadn't been hurt badly, mainly a few cuts and bruises, but it should have been a sign for them to turn around and climb the hell out of there. Like most hard-core spelunkers, they ignored the warning and went on. Andy was regretting that decision now.

"How you doing?"

Andy had a hard time not laughing at the stupid question posed by Jack, the lone teen among a group of thirty year olds. "I've been better," seemed like as good an answer as any, especially considering the fact that he had several broken ribs and a possible concussion.

"Not to alarm anyone, but we need to get out of here." Maggie looked tired and haggard, and she was the beauty of the group. Odd how flickering lights and mud can change a person's appearance.

Sam seemed to be the one taking charge, not by choice, but by necessity. "Does anyone have any suggestions on just how we do that?" His muscles bulged under his clothes as he stood there waiting for an answer. He was met with only silence.

Andy glanced around at this motley crew of cavers he had thrown in with. Most of them had made weekend trips like this before with him; yet, he could not honestly say that he knew any of them well enough to call them friends. They were simply people with the same interest who put up with each other in order to call themselves a group and go caving together. He barely knew the names of the other three men standing around him. To his great shame, he had no clue what the woman's name was that they'd lost. She had been new to the group and the least experienced. Why any of them had let her take the lead was beyond him.

Sam finally broke the awkward silence. "Obviously, we can not go back the way we came. This only leaves one alternative. We have to get back in the river."

"Are you crazy?" Maggie asked. "We have no idea where it goes or how dangerous it is. That river is the whole reason we are in trouble now."

This was not a statement Andy could disagree with. The river had been their folly. Climbing down the three tiers of cliff into the big room seemed tame by comparison now. It had been young Jack that decided they should leave the main passageway and check out some of the less traveled tunnels. They had crawled for several hundred feet before coming into a large room full of breakdown. That was when they heard the low rumble. It sounded like rapids. Realizing the group might have stumbled onto an underground river, all were excited as they made their way around the piles of broken rock and boulders. As the passage narrowed, they found themselves looking down a muddy slope into the pitch black darkness. Though none could see the water, its sound was unmistakable.

Andy laughed to himself. He had been the one to suggest they tie their ropes together before venturing farther. It seemed like a good idea at the time. The slope was steeper and slicker than any of them could have imagined. The new gal had ventured down it, with Andy directly behind her. In a split second they were both on their butts, sliding at high speed. The force of their weight brought the others down behind them. Luckily, the slope leveled out before dropping into the river. The group had found themselves on the muddy bank, intact and uninjured. After a bit of nervous laughter they gathered themselves together and tried to start up the steep slope. No one could climb it. Trying to hammer in a few spikes proved to be a futile effort. They kept pulling out of the soft mud.

Maggie's voice brought Andy back to their present predicament. "We lost Shelley in the river. Andy has some serious injuries from trying to save her. Do you really think we should risk any more of us getting hurt or killed?"

At least Andy felt better knowing he had a name for the woman now. Not that it was going to do her any good. He tried to sit up, ignoring the excruciating pain in his side.

"Are we certain this passage goes nowhere?"

Jack was shaking his head. "It turns into a crawl and then dead-ends. We have no choice at this point, but to go back to the river."

"I think we should avoid getting in the water again," Maggie adamantly stated.

Sam frowned. "We don't have a lot of other choices. Either we take a chance in the river or we sit down and die. Don't forget, nobody knows where we are. When none of us come home, they are going to be looking for us miles away from here."

"No matter what we decide, we should get out of this passage and back to the main one. At least by the river the rooms are bigger. Nobody would find us here, even if they were looking," Jack pointed out. The kid was smarter than some of the adults.

Sam leaned down to help Andy up. "Think you can make it back?"

"I made it from the river to here. Should be no problem getting back," Andy answered, taking the other man's hand and pulling himself to his feet.

The going was slow, but they made it back to where the river was roaring through a large passage. Andy sat back down and leaned against a large rock. The others seemed too impatient to take the time to sit and rest. Sam appeared troubled and several times went to huddle with the men, making sure Andy and Maggie did not hear the discussion. The lone woman amongst the group seemed content to be left out of the decision making. She simply paced back and forth in front of Andy.

"Don't be so hard on them. Sam is only trying to figure out how to get us rescued." Andy knew the guy well enough to know he didn't want to leave anyone behind. Even though at the moment, that made the most sense.

"I don't see how you could possibly want to get back in the water after what happened to you."

"I'm not getting back in the water yet," Andy replied. "When you guys send back a rescue party, I'll be ready to go then."

"What are you talking about? We aren't leaving you here."

Andy knew better. He had barely been able to walk. His injuries were internal. Being bounced around in the water and possibly smashed into more rocks was out of the question. The matter of time was also of great importance. The longer all of them stayed down there, the weaker they would become. Not to mention, disoriented. All of them were wet from their time in the river. Hypothermia was a sneaky devil that hit without warning. Andy wanted his companions to get out of the cave as quickly as possible and send him back medical help.

Maggie was not happy with the scenario in front of them. Andy could see it on her face as Sam and the others rejoined them. She let it be known. "We can't leave Andy behind."

"We never planned to," Sam stated. "I figure that I'm strong enough to keep hold of him once we get back in the current. Jack is going to tie himself on to us so that he can be my backup if something does happen."

Andy was going to have none of these heroics. "Like hell you are. I'm pretty sure I'm bleeding inside. Banging me up some more is not in my plans. The rest of you can make better time without being hobbled with a cripple. I want you to get out of here and send me back some proper help. There is no other way."

"I don't like the idea of splitting up," Sam stated. "Are you sure you can't make it in the river?"

"I don't think I could even get back up right now," Andy answered. "The best thing you can do for me is find a way out of this damned cave and get me rescued."

"One of us will have to stay then," Sam realized, "because it wouldn't be wise to leave an injured person alone down here."

Maggie frowned a bit before speaking. "I'll stay."

"No offense, Mags, but I'd prefer Jack stick with Andy. He's got a little more muscle than you. If we don't get back here by tomorrow Jack and Andy will need to chance the river on their own. Jack's a strong swimmer. It makes the most sense for him to stay." Sam knew the score.

"Why don't you all go? I don't need a babysitter," Andy insisted.

"Someone stays or we all stay." Sam was not a man to use his words lightly.

"Then leave the boy and get out of here," Andy conceded.

Maggie looked down at him with concern. "Are you sure you don't want me to stick around as well?"

Andy knew it was a hollow offer. She was wanting to get out of that cave as much as the rest of them. "Don't be silly. All I ask of you is to make sure we have a big, hot pizza waiting for us when we get out. Jack and I are going to be starving before this is over. Now get out of here. And be careful."

"You know we will," Maggie tried to grin. "Besides, what are the chances of there being another waterfall? This river has to come out somewhere."

"Hopefully, the exit is only around the corner," Andy laughed. "If it's that close, come back and get us."

"Will do."

Andy watched as the others got their gear together, leaving extra candles and batteries for him and Jack. They then slowly waded back into the swiftly moving current. The water was chest high on his companions as they vanished into the narrow passage. Their task was not one he'd wish on his worst enemy. None of them knew what lay ahead, leaving them to the mercy of the river. A river that had already taken one of their number.

"Care if I look around?" Jack asked. "I noticed some flowstone around the corner where we got out of the water. Thought there might be some small passages up above it. The water that formed them had to come from somewhere."

"A good observation," Andy agreed. "Take your time. I'll be fine."

Jack cautiously kept to the bank of the river as he rounded the bend, leaving Andy alone. A rush of quiet seemed to fill the vast chamber, even though the sound of the moving water was a constant. Andy pulled off his hardhat, placing it on a rock so that the light would illuminate the room better. His side was hurting again, but he was starting to get used to the pain. Wet clothes had brought about a numbing affect. He didn't know if that was good or bad. Fumbling in his pack, Andy found a candy bar. Chocolate would calm his nerves.

Why on earth had they gotten into the river? Andy would kick himself for that decision a long time. Everyone had been so excited about finding something new and unexplored. The water started out waist deep, but as the tunnel narrowed into a tight tube, the current grew swift enough to knock them off their feet, forcing them to swim along. By the time they realized their mistake, it was too late. The cavers were being bounced along into deep waters with no way out. The walls had been slippery, with nothing to catch onto. Shelley heard the roar first and tried to holler a warning back to the rest, but it had been useless. Even if they had wanted to, they couldn't get out.

Andy turned to see if Jack's light was in view. There was nothing but darkness coming from around the corner. He hoped the kid wasn't going to try to go back to the dome room. The rapids below the falls had been much too dangerous. He held his injured side, remembering the events that had brought him to this place.

Shelley had been catapulted over the waterfall. Realizing what was immediately ahead, Andy was able to use the rope that tied them all together, and toss it around a huge boulder at the top of the falls as he went over. This was the only thing that saved their lives. The others were pulled to the other side of the waterfall, which just happened to be more of a cascade. Andy and Shelley were hanging with a forty foot drop below them, and taking the full brunt of the forceful waters. They were all in a precarious predicament. Andy knew by the dead weight below him that Shelley wasn't conscious. He had to do something and do it quickly. Grabbing his knife from the sheath on his belt, he reached up and cut the rope. All he heard was the screams of the others as he fell into a black abyss of water.

It was a miracle that his hardhat and light stayed on his head. He had come up out of the water to find himself fighting the powerful undertow of the waterfall. Upon seeing his predicament, Andy swam as hard as he could away from the turbulent wall of water. The move put him right into the rapids. Andy then had seen the woman who'd fallen with him. She had regained consciousness and was struggling frantically as the raging river pulled her around in circles. Andy realized she was caught in some sort of whirlpool. He rushed to her rescue. The river had other ideas. The rapids smashed Andy into several large boulders, pulling him down the main passage and away from the swirling pool. All Andy could do was watch helplessly as the woman was sucked under the water. She did not come back up.

The others had apparently come down the cascading side of the falls, making it more like a waterslide. They too were dumped into the main current and swept down the massive passage toward Andy. None of them could seem to escape the raging river as it swept them out of the huge, dome shaped room. It wasn't until a quarter of a mile later that the rapids let up. They had come around a curve to find themselves in another big room. A room with lots of riverbank and dry land. A place from which they would make decisions that would decide all their fates.

Andy tried to stand, but the pain was too much. He leaned back against the rock. How long had the others been gone he wondered? Jack should have returned by then. He glanced back in the direction the boy had gone. The thought of hollering for the kid crossed his mind, but he decided against it. Maybe the teen had found a passage out. There was no sense in panicking just yet. Andy decided to take the opportunity to rest a bit. He carefully lay down across the soft, dirt floor, using his pack for a pillow. The events of the day had taken their toll. Andy was fast asleep in moments.

Darkness. Nothing but total black. Andy wasn't even sure if his eyes were open or closed. He wondered how long he'd slept? When had the light gone out? All he could hear was the sound of rushing water nearby. He sat up. Weakness had overcome him, but he still found the strength to search around in his pack for a source of light. All the matches were still wet, but he had a flashlight with fresh batteries. It didn't come on. The river had not been kind to his equipment. He frantically felt around for some candles. There were three of them. All he needed to do was wait for the matches to dry and then he'd have light again. He found himself trying to remember if Jack had taken the pack with the spare supplies or if they were nearby in the darkness. Andy decided not to move around unless it became totally necessary. He found a granola bar and ate it.

Seconds turn to minutes, and minutes into hours. Beneath the ground in total darkness, hours seem like days. Andy drifted in and out of sleep, never actually certain of when or if he was awake. His only solace was that the others had made it out and any minute a rescue party would arrive. It wasn't until he ran out of food that he started to get worried. He had only eaten when he knew hunger was about to get the best of him. None of the matches would light. The black void all around him was becoming unbearable. In the grasp of darkness he found himself unable to move from where he sat. Fear of getting too near the river or hitting his head against the rocks kept him from checking the area to see if the other pack was still around. So he sat and sat and sat.

Andy began painting pictures in his mind as to what might have befallen his companions. What if the river never came back out to the surface? Underground rivers could go for hundreds of miles. Maggie, Sam and the others could have easily been swept into deep waters and pulled under. Or they might have hit more dangerous rapids. Another waterfall was unlikely, but not completely out of the question either. He didn't even want to think about the whirlpool that Shelley had vanished into. There could obviously be vast underwater passages beneath them. That could also explain why Jack had never returned. Maybe he somehow made it back to the dome room, but got caught in the whirlpool. Or he could have found some new crawl passage and gotten stuck. Andy realized he might never know what became of the others.

The loss of hope is the greatest obstacle of all. Andy lay down and closed his eyes. The river had dealt a losing hand. The darkness beneath had won.

THE BOY WHO NEVER SAW SNOW

Timmy was so tired. Not in a physical way, that he had learned to live with. He was just tired of always being in the hospital. From the moment he had been born, Timmy knew no other life. Ten years of constantly being ill can take its toll on a kid. The endless visits to the emergency room, a sea of faces blurring by as doctors and nurses came and went, medicines that didn't work. Always being monitored and cared for. Timmy was sick of it all.

There was only one thing keeping him alive. Never having left Miami, he had never seen snow. It was the one dream that kept him going. Timmy had come to the realization that he wasn't going to ever get better; it was his mother who couldn't come to grips with that fact. She was ever present at his side. Her marriage had collapsed under the pressure of ignoring all others to care for her sick son. Timmy had never blamed his dad for leaving. He just wished he could have visited more, but he had remarried and was now expecting another child. It was hard to get away from a second family. Tina was the one Timmy felt most sorry for. His big sister lost all the attention at the age of three when he was born. Although she never said a word, he knew she resented him. She had been ignored by their parents for years. He wouldn't be surprised if she even hated him. If it would only snow, Timmy thought to himself.

***

Norma found herself watching the monitor at the foot of her son's bed. What a way to spend a Christmas Eve. She had almost forgotten what it was like to spend a normal holiday with family and friends. As much as she hated admitting it, her heart had grown bitter. Christmas didn't mean much to her anymore. How could a loving God let her sweet little boy endure such suffering? She had lost her faith a long time ago. Even before her husband had left.

The thought of him and his new wife having a child really angered her. How could the man be so thoughtless? He had a sick son he seldom visited and a teenage daughter who was constantly shuttled back and forth between them. It wasn't right that he was about to enjoy happiness again. It wasn't fair.

"Can I come in?" Speak of the devil, Norma thought to herself as her ex stood at the doorway. "How is he doing? Janet and I wanted to bring him his presents tonight."

"Why would you bring them now? Aren't you planning on spending tomorrow here with us?" Norma asked, trying to keep the anger out of her voice.

"Change of plans. We are going to Janet's folks for Christmas. I think Timmy will understand."

Norma wanted to pound her fist into the man's face until she noticed his new wife standing out in the hall. Seeing the pregnant woman redirected her fury. "What is she doing here? Shouldn't she be in bed? Or isn't that how she got in her condition to begin with?"

"Leave her out of this! You and I were done long before I met her. Stop trying to insinuate she had something to do with our breaking up. You know as well as I do what brought that about." His tone let her know to drop the subject. She hated it when he was right.

"I'm sorry, David." Norma looked toward the pregnant woman behind him. "I really didn't mean what I said Janet. This has been a bad day. Timmy took a turn for the worse this afternoon and my nerves are frazzled. Where is Tina?"

"She didn't want to come, so we left her at the house. Before you get mad about what I am going to ask, please consider how Tina feels. She wants to come with us tomorrow instead of here to the hospital. Janet's family has said she is more than welcomed to join us."

"Please let her go, mom." Norma turned to see that Timmy had awakened. "She hates hospital food. Let her go have a nice dinner with dad."

David and Janet both came into the room and moved next to the bed. Timmy tried to sit up, but was too weak. Norma rushed around to his side and fixed the pillow up underneath his head, allowing him to look at his visitors. She couldn't understand how her son, even at his lowest point, could be so unselfish. He was always trying to calm everyone else around him. She knew his heart had to be breaking at the thought of spending another Christmas in the hospital, yet, he wasn't the least bit angry that his father and sister didn't want to spend it with him. She wondered how such a good boy could have so many bad things happen to him. From the day Timmy was born there was always a smile on his face. Throughout all the operations and transfusions, what had remained a constant, was his joyful spirit. This caring, loving child only wanted others to be happy.

"If it is what you really want, honey," Norma tried to smile through the tears.

"Why don't you go too? It would be good for you to have Christmas in a house again."

Norma had to put her hand to her mouth to keep from crying. "Your sister can go, but I'm not leaving you here to have the holiday by yourself. I'll be right by your side as we watch the parade on television and then have a nice meal with the nurses."

"Maybe I should stay," David added, taking his son by the hand. "We can do the home thing next year."

Timmy looked at him with pleading eyes. "Please don't stay because of me. I want you to go. Tina needs to see what it is like to have a real Christmas. Besides, I already know what I want for next year."

Norma was stunned by this sudden revelation. He had asked for nothing from her. "Are you sure we can't get it for you this year?"

Timmy smiled weakly. "I want to see snow. The real stuff. Not on TV. One of the nurses brought me this brochure for some cabins in Colorado. Can we go there next Christmas?"

"I'm not sure the doctors would agree to let you take such a strenuous trip," David started. Norma shot him a serious look.

"Maybe we could hire someone to bring a snow machine here to the hospital," she suggested.

Timmy shook his head. "It wouldn't be the same. I want to see the real stuff. No matter what happens, you have to promise me we'll go to Colorado next year for Christmas. All of us. I want my mom and dad and sister there. And my new step-mom and baby."

He had never asked for anything for himself, and now he was asking for the impossible, Norma thought. She wondered how David was going to wiggle his way out of this one? Timmy had grown used to his dad's infrequent visits, but he had never asked him for a promise. She watched as her ex-husband glanced at his new wife and then turned back to the boy.

"I promise you, we will all be playing in the snow next year. I'll book us a cabin in the mountains just for you. But you have to promise to try and get stronger so that we can build a snowman together. Is it a deal?"

Timmy's face lit up like never before as David bent down and hugged him. "You made a promise, dad. Not just to me, but also for mom and Tina."

"We'll all be there together. Now you get some more rest and I'll be back soon. There is something I've got to do. We'll open your presents when I return."

"Don't forget, you promised." Timmy smiled.

Norma watched as David and Janet left the room. She pulled a chair over next to the bed and held her son's hand. "I never knew you wanted to see snow so much. Why didn't you tell me?"

"It is just something I've never seen and I always wanted too. I thought if I told you, it would only make you sad."

"Why did you think that?"

"Because you would have known I would never see it. The doctors will never let me go that far away."

Norma put up her hand to emphasize, "They will have a hard time keeping you in this bed next year. If you want to see snow, then you are going to see snow. I don't care what the doctors say."

A huge grin crossed Timmy's ashen face. "Can we eat snowflakes?"

"As many as you like until your tummy is full."

"Will you show me how to make a snow Angel?"

"We'll make them all around the cabin."

"I love you, mommy." Timmy closed his eyes and fell asleep.

Norma wiped the tears from her eyes as she leaned back against the chair and found herself staring at the monitor again. She realized it wasn't working as she got up and went over to make sure it was on. The stupid thing had stopped. She was about to call for a nurse when the sudden realization of the situation hit her. A cry of anguish escaped her lips as she rushed to the bed. Cradling her son in her arms, Norma rocked back and forth, unable to let his lifeless body go. She knew he was gone, but she was still in a state of disbelief. Her sweet boy would have no more pain. That now belonged to her.

"We decided to stick around for tomorrow," David said, walking into the room with Janet close behind. He was holding a snow globe in his hand.

Norma looked at them through a sea of tears. "He's gone. Our Angel never got to see snow."

***

The Rocky Mountains were spectacular in winter. A dusting of snow covered the jagged crags of the peaks. Norma stepped out of the cabin, glancing around at the scenery that surrounded her. It was still hard for her to believe that Timmy had been gone a year. Not a day went by that her heart was not breaking. With his passing, she had given up on life. The only thing that had made her agree to come on this trip was the constant pleading of her daughter to keep Timmy's promise. Norma knew David had been just as hesitant as herself. She had to commend the man for pulling through and making their son's dream a reality.

David and Janet had rented a cozy cabin in the woods near Leadville. Three of the tallest mountains in Colorado could be seen from the porch. Norma had tried to bow out of the trip, letting Tina go alone, but they all made it clear that she had to come as well. Even Janet had gone out of her way to let Norma know she was welcomed. Not too many wives would want the husband's ex along for a winter vacation. Of course most of Janet's time was taken up with caring for the baby. The child had been born the day after Christmas. With the funeral for Timmy the following day, no one had been more surprised than Norma when Janet pulled herself out of the hospital and attended.

"Mom, can we go for a walk?" Tina asked, coming out onto the porch. "Little Robby is down for a nap and I think dad and Janet want to use the chance to rest."

Norma tried to smile. "Are you sure you can maneuver through all this snow? I was noticing how much there is of it."

Tina laughed, "Don't be silly, mom. There are only a few inches on the ground."

"Which is more than I've ever seen before," Norma pointed out. She was a Florida girl through and through.

The fourteen year old ran down the steps and grabbed a big handful of the white stuff. "If you don't walk with me, I'll throw this at you."

"I'm coming," Norma smiled as she stepped from the porch. "If you dare throw a snowball at me, I am turning around and going back in that cabin and I won't set foot outside for the rest of this trip."

Tina smiled, letting the snow fall from her hand. "I wonder if Timmy had any idea that snow was so cold?"

Norma had to compose herself. The mere mention of her son's name made her miss him even more. Because Tina had seldom mentioned her brother in the past year, Norma knew better than to get upset, for fear it would make Tina try to forget all about him. "He would have loved to see the mountains covered in snow. Look at all the pine trees. They look like a Christmas card."

The two of them walked down the path in silence. Norma wondered how much her daughter missed Timmy? The girl had held so much in during the final days. As much as Norma wanted to talk with her about it, she could never seem to find the right words to get a conversation going. Tina had spent more and more time with her father and his new family. Under the best of conditions, Norma might have resented it, but with being in a constant state of sorrow, she had found relief in the fact that Tina was able to escape to a happier place. The new baby had greatly taken everyone's mind away from the loss of Timmy. Everyone that is except Norma. She had refused to hold the newborn child, constantly making excuses as to why. Robby was a cute baby, but he would never replace her beloved son.

"How are you holding up, mom?" Tina finally asked. "I know tonight is Christmas Eve and how hard it is going to be for you. Dad said he has been dreading this night all year long."

"Have you talked with your father about Timmy?"

Tina took her mother by the hand. "We talk about him all the time. I wish you would. Timmy loved you more than anyone, yet you hardly ever mention him without crying. That is why I seldom talk about him around you, but I like remembering the fun things about him, not the sad ones. Timmy loved to smile more than anyone I've ever known. I think that is what I miss about him the most."

The realization that this was her chance to open up and share with her daughter was almost more than Norma could take. Now that the door was unlocked, she wasn't sure she could open it. Fighting back the tears was hard. "For such a little boy, he had such a big heart. I miss his smile too. He always wanted everyone else to be happy."

Hugging her mother, Tina said, "I felt so guilty sometimes for being healthy. Timmy was always apologizing to me for his being sick. He thought I hated him because he got all the attention. I never blamed him. It was you and dad I was mad at. I could see you getting sadder and sadder as Timmy got sicker. Then dad left because he couldn't stand the sadness. He ran away from all of us."

"I could kill your father," Norma started to say.

Tina broke in. "But don't you see, mom. You are doing the same thing. Can't you see that you are running away from life? Timmy is gone, but I'm still here. Doesn't that matter to you?"

"My sweet darling, of course it does." Norma hugged her daughter tightly. "I'd give anything to stop missing your brother, but I can't. All I can think about is the fact that he never got to see the snow. If I could have only made that one wish come true for him, I think I could have gotten over his loss. As it is, I feel like I let him down and failed. Nothing is going to change that."

"I wish you had told me this sooner, mom. You never failed Timmy. I think he knew he would never see snow. He only wanted you to see it for him. And now that you are here, you have done what he wanted."

"If it was only that simple."

Before either of them had a chance to speak, the rented van came around the corner. Norma pulled away from her daughter to wipe the tears from her cheeks. She didn't want the others to see she had been crying. Tina jumped up and down as David pulled the vehicle to a stop and opened the door. He stepped out and grinned at them both. "How about coming with me to town. I want to get us a tree to decorate before it gets too late. They say another front is coming in and we might get more snow tonight." He sounded so cheerful.

"Can we get an Angel for the top?" Tina begged, opening the passenger door and getting in.

"Are you coming?" David asked.

Norma shook her head. "I don't really feel like going to town. Why don't you two go on without me. I'll walk on back to the cabin and see what needs to be done for dinner."

"Want a ride back? It's no trouble to turn the van around," David offered.

"Don't be silly. It's not very far. Go get the tree and some decorations. If you have time, pick up another carton of whip topping. I'm not sure we'll have enough for all the pies."

"Will do. Janet and Robby are awake, so don't say I didn't warn you," David laughed, getting back inside the vehicle.

Norma watched as the two of them drove off down the muddy road. She found comfort in the fact that Tina and David had been able to talk with one another after Timmy had died. Her daughter had obviously been the one with the most insight into how each of them had dealt with the loss. Norma knew Tina was the strongest of them all. Maybe that was why they had let her go her own way. She had never seemed to need either one of them. Norma could see that she and David needed Tina. A light snow began to fall as she traipsed back to the cabin. Hopefully, David had started a fire before leaving. Noticing smoke coming from the chimney answered her question. She was ready for a nice hot cup of coffee.

"Norma! Robby has something stuck in his throat!" Janet was screaming as she ran out onto the porch with the little boy in her arms.

By the terror stricken look on the woman's face, Norma knew the worst thing to do was panic. She ran up the steps and grabbed the baby from the other woman. Instinctively, she turned the boy over on his stomach, holding him across her arm, pointing his head downward. Robby was gasping for breath as his tiny body shuddered. Norma slapped him a couple of times on the back before putting her finger down his throat. She felt the plastic ball pop forward and was able to quickly pull it out of his mouth. A loud cry erupted from the child as Norma turned him back around and held him against her shoulder.

"Is he all right?" Janet sobbed, reaching for her son.

"He'll be fine," Norma assured her as she handed the boy back to his mother. "Let's get him back inside so he doesn't catch cold out here."

"I feel so stupid. I had only turned around for a second and he was into the toys. This is terrible. You must think I'm an awful mother for not watching him better than this." Janet was a bundle of nerves as they both went into the cabin.

"Not at all. Every kid I've known likes to put things in their mouth that they shouldn't. Timmy swallowed some marbles one time and about gave me a fit. You don't want to know how they came out!"

"Thank you so much for being here. I don't know what I would have done without you," Janet stated.

"Well, now you know what to do if it ever happens again. Don't blame yourself, kids are going to get into stuff. You just need to be ready to get them out."

Janet suddenly seemed calmer. "I think that is the first

time you've ever held Robby."

Norma tried not to look her in the eyes. "Don't be silly. I'm sure I've held him before." She also knew that wasn't exactly the truth.

Janet held the boy toward her. "Can you please take him for me so I can go collect myself? I can't stop shaking."

Norma took the child in her arms. He was still sobbing. Robby grabbed her finger tightly and let a faint smile cross his face. The little boy had blue eyes. Norma had never noticed before. She held him close to her as Janet went into the other room. Before she knew it, the boy was laughing, having forgotten all about his previous ordeal. Making faces at the child sent him into a giggling frenzy. A sense of guilt swept through her thoughts. Here she was enjoying the company of a little boy that was not her Timmy. The moment weighed heavy on her soul.

"Look at you two, getting along like old friends," Janet noted upon her return.

"He's a handsome little boy. You and David should be proud of yourselves. Cherish every moment." Norma handed the boy back to Janet. "I'm going to get dinner started. You play with your son and don't argue with me about this. There is no need to mention what happened to the others either. No sense in getting them worried about something that has already happened. Robby is fine and that is all that matters. Now, I am going to cook and I prefer having the kitchen to myself. Besides, most of the food has already been prepared and only needs to be heated up. I'll holler if I need help with anything."

"Are you sure?" Janet obviously wanted to assist in the kitchen.

"I promise, if I need anything, you'll know it. Now go enjoy that fire and play with Robby."

Norma made herself busy, trying to ignore how happy she had felt to hold a child in her arms again. It was a feeling she had almost let herself forget. The smell of pumpkin pie filtered through the small cabin. Many years had gone by since she had last cooked up a holiday meal for her family. She was almost done when David and Tina returned with a tree for decorating.

"Wasn't too smart to wait so late," David laughed as he brought in a rather small fir tree. "Apparently, even in Colorado they can run out of big trees. Hope this one will do?"

Tina was all smiles as she came through the door, carrying a box of ornaments. Norma went over and gave her a hug. Janet and Robby joined them. The baby seemed to light up at the sight of all the brightly colored balls in the box. Norma looked over to see Janet looking at her. A smile passed between them.

"The food really smells good," David noted, after setting up the tree near the fireplace.

"Norma has been in the kitchen all afternoon. I tried to help, but she wouldn't let me," Janet pointed out.

"Have you looked outside? The snow is really coming down fast," Tina told them. "After we eat, can we go make a snowman?"

"If it's not too dark. I don't see why not," David smiled. "Should we dress up the tree before or after we eat? You ladies are in charge."

Janet gave him a quick kiss on the cheek. "The decision should be Norma's since she did all the work."

"I'll put it this way," Norma began, "the ham won't be done for another thirty minutes."

Tina yelled, "That gives us plenty of time."

Norma watched as her daughter and David went to the

task of trimming the tree. They had it finished in no time. Tina wanted to put the Angel on herself. After she had placed it on the top of the tree, she turned around and smiled at everyone. "This is for Timmy."

"Well said," David agreed. Norma thought she saw a tear in his eye. "Let's go eat."

The meal was delicious. Norma realized she had outdone herself this time. Between compliments from the others, she found herself making funny faces at Robby in his high-chair. It never occurred to her how surprising this was to Tina and David. She knew they never expected her to have anything to do with the boy, but that had all changed that afternoon. Norma picked Robby up from his seat and carried him over to the tree. The child reached out to touch the sparkling ornaments as Norma softly hummed a Christmas tune to him.

"I never thought I'd see that," David leaned over and whispered to his wife, but in the small cabin, he was heard by all.

"Isn't my new baby brother a cutie?" Tina asked, joining her mother at the tree. She tickled Robby's chin.

"Very much so," Norma smiled as Tina put her arm around her.

"I'm so glad we came, mom."

"Me too."

"Grab your coats everybody. Let's go outside and enjoy the snow." David seemed relieved to finally see Norma holding his son.

After getting into warmer clothes, they all ventured outside. The last rays of daylight were almost a memory as giant flakes fell from the sky. Tina ran out and jumped into a drift of snow. Janet had taken Robby and was letting him try to walk in the soft whiteness. The boy didn't know what to make of it. David stood close to Norma watching as his children played.

"You married well," Norma finally broke the silence. "Janet is a wonderful human being. Robby is a beautiful child. I'm glad you are finally happy."

There was a long pause before David spoke. "I married well both times, Norma. You were my first love and you always will be. I'm so sorry I let you and the children down, but I couldn't deal with Timmy's illness. It tore me up every time I had to see him in that hospital. I felt like I wasn't just losing him, but you as well. Nothing could pull you away from his side. In the end, I became jealous of my own son. All your love and compassion seemed to go to only him. Then I hated myself for thinking such thoughts. I loved Timmy so much. He was truly an Angel on earth. Can you ever forgive me for being so cowardly and selfish?"

Norma wept softly to herself. "I never knew you felt that way. I only thought you didn't care anymore. Can you ever forgive me for being such an awful person?"

"Don't ever say that. You did more than your share. We are both to blame for not making enough time for Tina. Can we forgive each other for the past mistakes and try to make a better future for her?"

All she had to do was look into his eyes and she knew all was forgiven between them. Norma squeezed David's hand before wiping tears from her eyes once again. Crying all the time was a habit she was ready to break. Norma ran over to where Tina was building a small snowman. She glanced back to see David hugging his wife and baby. That was as it should be she realized.

"Mom, what do you think Timmy would have wanted to do first if he could have been here with us?" Tina asked.

A few days before and that question would have made Norma burst into tears, but being able to talk about Timmy again with the ones who had loved him most had brought her mind a sense of peace. "One of the last things he told me was that he wanted to make a snow Angel. Why don't we all make them?" She turned to Janet and David. "Come join us. We are going to make Angels in the snow."

"I haven't done that since I was a kid," Janet laughed as she and David made their way over to the snow bank.

"At least you've done it before. None of us has ever been near this much snow. Show us how it is done," Norma prompted in a friendly voice.

Janet handed Robby to David before turning around and falling back into the snow. She then proceeded to move her arms and legs back and forth. "Now help me up," she begged. Norma and Tina each gave her a hand as she came to her feet. She then pointed back to her masterpiece. "That is how you do it."

Norma was impressed at the image left behind in the snow. It truly did look like an Angel. She turned to Tina. "Let's put ours next to hers." They both fell into the snow laughing as they made their images. Janet took Robby so that David could help them get back up.

"Now it is your turn," Tina told her father, pulling him to a spot next to hers.

"And lets not forget about little Robby," Norma implored, "He should be next to his daddy."

David lay down in the snow as the women put the infant beside him. "Do what I do." To everyone's surprise, the boy made a perfect Angel image.

"Snow," Robby yelled out very clearly. He was all smiles as his parents swept him up in their embrace.

Norma knew it was a special moment. She was suddenly glad that she had gotten to be a part of it. If only Timmy could have been there. He would have so loved to be playing in the snow and watching his family be together as they should have been. She realized the new baby brother would have been his pride and joy. Timmy would have shown Robby all the things he never got to experience himself. If only it could have been.

The snow stopped falling as a few twinkling stars shone through the clouds above. The panoramic majesty of the mountains seemed to glow all around them. They all pulled together and helped Tina finish her snowman. As they were getting ready to return to the warmth of the cabin, Norma thought she heard a familiar laugh from off in the distance. She turned toward the spot they had all made their snow Angels.

"Did you hear it too?" Tina asked. "It sounded just like Timmy."

Norma thought her heart was going to stop when she realized they had all heard the same thing. She had been willing to think it was her imagination until Tina had spoken. The five of them made their way to the Angels and then stopped in their tracks. Another image was now in the snow above theirs. It was about the size of a ten year old boy. And there was one thing that none of them could help but notice. There were no other tracks or footprints anywhere near the image. Norma could feel it in the air on this glorious Christmas Eve. The Angel that had left his image was her Timmy. Her heart was filled with such joy at the knowledge that he was now among the Angels and resting in the arms of God. This was indeed, going to be a Merry Christmas.

DIFFERENT DIRECTIONS

Though I tend to go
In many different directions
I always seem
To find myself
Coming back
To the place
I call home

For the further adventures of Enyaw Nhoj and his ship, the Marie-Alena, look for the up-coming, full length fantasy tale from Sonny Collins.

THE OCEAN ROAD

About the Author

Sonny Collins was born and raised in Oklahoma where he nurtured his love of hiking, camping, caving and all things to do with the great outdoors. Now splitting his time between properties in Kansas and Colorado, he is an avid traveler and wilderness explorer. Although photography is his great passion, writing poetry and telling stories are simply a part of his very being.

After the publication of his first two books, Sonny made the decision to devote more time to his writing in the serious pursuit of finding a following among readers. His next two collections were of poetry, which were received favorably and became the top-selling books for Prairie Moon Publications. A jab at playwriting soon followed. With this, his sixth work, Sonny has realized his dream of mixing all genres together into one single collection of short stories.

Sonny does not consider himself a writer, but a storyteller. After reading this eclectic group of tales, you decide.

Prairie Moon Publications
P. O. Box 236
Hillsboro, KS 67063

www.ingramcontent.com/pod-product-compliance
Lightning Source LLC
Chambersburg PA
CBHW032010240626
47153CB00003B/1192